Cowboy at Heart

SHIPMENT FIVE

Belonging to Bandera by Tina Leonard
Court Me, Cowboy by Barbara White Daille
His Best Friend's Bride by Jodi O'Donnell
The Cowboy's Return by Linda Warren
Baby Be Mine by Victoria Pade
The Cattle Baron by Margaret Way

SHIPMENT SIX

Crockett's Seduction by Tina Leonard
Coming Home to the Cattleman by Judy Christenberry
Almost Perfect by Judy Duarte
Cowboy Dad by Cathy McDavid
Real Cowboys by Roz Denny Fox
The Rancher Wore Suits by Rita Herron
Falling for the Texas Tycoon by Karen Rose Smith

SHIPMENT SEVEN

Last's Temptation by Tina Leonard
Daddy by Choice by Marin Thomas
The Cowboy, the Baby and the Bride-to-Be by Cara Colter
Luke's Proposal by Lois Faye Dyer
The Truth About Cowboys by Margot Early
The Other Side of Paradise by Laurie Paige

SHIPMENT EIGHT

Mason's Marriage by Tina Leonard
Bride at Briar's Ridge by Margaret Way
Texas Bluff by Linda Warren
Cupid and the Cowboy by Carol Finch
The Horseman's Son by Delores Fossen
Cattleman's Bride-to-Be by Lois Faye Dyer

**The rugged, masculine and independent men
of America's West know the value of hard work,
honor and family. They may be ranchers, tycoons
or the guy next door, but they're all cowboys at heart.
Don't miss any of the books in this collection!**

Cowboy
at
Heart

TAMING A DARK HORSE
STELLA BAGWELL
USA TODAY Bestselling Author

HARLEQUIN® COWBOY AT HEART

If you purchased this book without a cover you should be aware
that this book is stolen property. It was reported as "unsold and
destroyed" to the publisher, and neither the author nor the
publisher has received any payment for this "stripped book."

Recycling programs
for this product may
not exist in your area.

ISBN-13: 978-0-373-82610-0

TAMING A DARK HORSE

Copyright © 2005 by Stella Bagwell

All rights reserved. Except for use in any review, the reproduction or
utilization of this work in whole or in part in any form by any electronic,
mechanical or other means, now known or hereafter invented, including
xerography, photocopying and recording, or in any information storage
or retrieval system, is forbidden without the written permission of the
publisher, Harlequin Enterprises Limited, 225 Duncan Mill Road,
Don Mills, Ontario M3B 3K9, Canada.

This is a work of fiction. Names, characters, places and incidents are
either the product of the author's imagination or are used fictitiously,
and any resemblance to actual persons, living or dead, business
establishments, events or locales is entirely coincidental.

This edition published by arrangement with Harlequin Books S.A.

For questions and comments about the quality of this book,
please contact us at CustomerService@Harlequin.com.

® and TM are trademarks of Harlequin Enterprises Limited or its
corporate affiliates. Trademarks indicated with ® are registered in the
United States Patent and Trademark Office, the Canadian Trade Marks
Office and in other countries.

Printed in U.S.A.

H HARLEQUIN®
™ www.Harlequin.com

STELLA BAGWELL

has written more than seventy novels for Harlequin and Silhouette Books. She is grateful to her loyal readers and hopes her stories have brightened their lives in some small way. A cowgirl through and through, she loves to watch old Westerns, and has recently learned how to rope a steer. Her days begin and end helping her husband care for a beloved herd of horses on their little ranch located on the south Texas coast. When she's not ropin' and ridin', you'll find her at her desk, creating her next tale of love. The couple has a son, who is a high school math teacher and athletic coach. Stella loves to hear from readers and invites them to contact her at stellabagwell@gmail.com.

To our own beloved horses:
Thunder, Trouble, Spider John, Diamond,
Rooster, Topper, Shy Girl, Badger, Miss Kitty,
Potion, Major Bob, Festus, Newly, Doll Brown,
Sante Fe Solid, Maggie and the baby on the way.
And also in loving memory of Gus,
my brother's great trail horse.

Chapter One

"A nurse! Hell no! I don't need a nurse! I just need to get out of here!"

Linc Ketchum's loud protest rattled around the small hospital room. Normally he considered himself a quiet, unobtrusive guy, but since the terrible fire at the T Bar K horse barn two weeks ago he'd turned into a growling bear.

His tall, graying doctor gave him a stern look. "Sorry, Mr. Ketchum, but your hands and arms were badly burned and unless I'm assured that a nurse will be with you at all times, I cannot release you from this hospital. And that means round the clock. You're still highly susceptible to infection and I don't want any sort of pressure placed on your hands before they heal completely.

Your bandages will have to be changed routinely and your skin dressed. I want to know that it's done correctly."

Linc looked up at Dr. Olstead. "Hell, doc, if you're going to force me to have a nurse underfoot, I might as well stay in the hospital."

"I can certainly arrange that. As far as I'm concerned I'd rather have you here. But your family seems to think you'll heal better at home."

Grimacing, Linc glanced down at the sheets covering the lower half of his body. Except for short walks down the hall and sitting for brief spells in an armchair, he'd been stuck in this bed for too long. His whole body was beginning to ache. And that was just the physical side of things. Staring at the close, pale-green walls and the small television screen hanging in one corner of the room was enough to send him to the psychiatric ward. If he didn't get out of here soon he was going to start yelling and never stop.

"All right, doc. Whatever you say. If I

have to have a nurse—well, guess there's not much I can do about it. At least I'll be getting out of here." He lifted his heavily bundled hands and arms. The stiff white objects reminded him of a couple of pesky tree stumps in an otherwise clean pasture. If he had to button his jeans without assistance, or walk out of the hospital naked, he'd be forced to choose the latter. "I want to get out of this mess, doc. I want to get back to work."

"I'm going to cut the bandaging down soon," the doctor assured him, "but it will be at least two or three more weeks before I'll even consider allowing you to go back to work."

Linc opened his mouth to protest, but the doctor jumped in before he could say a word and went on to discuss the do's and don'ts he wanted Linc to stick to once he was released from the hospital.

When the man finally left the room, Linc was overwhelmed and just a little angry at being put in such a vulnerable state. He was a man who had never needed or asked for anything. He took care of himself and had done so from the time he was a teenager. He didn't like depending on other people for anything. But it appeared as though in the coming days he was going to have to do a lot of things he didn't like.

The memories of the fire that had brought him here suddenly welled up in Linc's head. He saw flames ripping at the walls of the horse barn and licking at the gates to each stable, the terrified horses rearing and pawing as they tried to escape the fire closing in around them. Their frightened squeals and whinnies had mixed with the loud roar of the crackling flames and the horrible sound still continued to wake Linc from his sleep. And though he tried to forget, he couldn't get anything about that nightmarish night out of his mind.

Time after time, he'd run back into the burning barn, grabbing every mare that he could and opening stall gates that were being eaten up by the creeping fire. The only thing he had to be thankful for was that all his beloved horses had gotten out safely. Only one had been slightly burned and his cousin Ross had assured him that she was well on the mend. As for Linc, the ordeal had pretty much cooked his hands and arms. But when he thought of his mares and colts and stallion, he knew saving them was worth every second of the pain he was going through now.

"Well, we've finally gotten some good news," Ross said now as he and his sister Victoria entered the room. "At least you're getting out of here tomorrow. That's something to look forward to."

Ross Ketchum was Linc's cousin. The two of them were almost the same age and had grown up together on the Ketchum's T Bar K ranch. They shared the responsibilities of running the multi-million-dollar operation. In spite of Ross being talkative and outgoing and Linc liking his privacy, the two of them were more like brothers than anything else. They even shared the same physical characteristics: long legs, a lean torso full of muscles, dark-brown hair and green eyes. Only, Linc's hair was lighter than Ross's and his eyes a much darker, muddier green.

"Yeah," Linc mumbled. "But where the hell am I going to go? I'd drive the boys in the bunkhouse crazy and I can't have a nurse wandering around a bunch of naked cowboys in the mornings. Unless it was a male nurse."

Victoria Hastings, Ross's sister and a practicing medical doctor, looked at him and laughed. "I don't think any nurse would be welcome in the bunkhouse."

"Only if it was Nurse Goodbody," Ross jokingly interjected.

Victoria rolled her eyes toward the ceiling. "Ross, our cousin doesn't need a Nurse Goodbody. He needs good care and rest."

"And that's just what he's going to get, sis." Standing at the head of Linc's bed, Ross grinned down at him. "As soon as he moves into the big house with me and Bella."

"Oh no! That's your place. I'm not butting in."

The main ranch house had been built nearly fifty years earlier by Linc's father, Randolf, and Ross's father, Tucker. Back then, the two Ketchum men had been partners, each of them owning half of the T Bar K, a spread that covered several sections in northwestern New Mexico. Initially, both men and their wives had lived together in the monstrous house built of rock and logs. But eventually Randolf had developed heart disease, sold his half to his brother and built a modest house across the ridge from the main estate.

His cousins Seth, Ross and Victoria had always treated Linc as a sibling. All three of them had insisted he always have access to the Ketchum house and the ranch's funds just as if he were their brother. Linc had always been grateful for their generosity, but he'd never taken advantage of it. He was his own man. And he wanted to be able to say he'd earned what he had by hard work, not by handouts.

"Damn it, Linc. The house is yours, too," Ross said now. "It belongs to all of us. Bella and I just happen to be living in it. And you don't have to be told there's plenty of empty rooms in the place. In fact, there's so many Bella doesn't know what to do with them."

Mutiny tightened Linc's jaw as he looked up at his cousin. "You can fill those empty rooms with kids. That would be a damn sight better than hosting a helpless cowboy who can't even button his own jeans."

Ross chuckled. "We're *trying* to fill them with kids, Linc. But that takes time, you know. It will take us a while to fill that many rooms."

"Well, I'm not going to be underfoot," Linc grumbled. "You and Bella are still newlyweds, you need to be alone."

"Tell that to Marina," Victoria wryly interjected.

Marina had been the cook-housekeeper for the Ketchum family since Linc and his cousins had been born. The large Hispanic woman knew more about all of them than they did themselves. She had an extra soft spot for Ross and didn't make any bones about showing it. Nor did she worry about speaking her mind. And no doubt she would demand to help care for Linc.

"That's another thing," Ross quickly put in. "In the big house Marina will be available to the nurse and—"

"No!" Linc interrupted. "Marina already has too much to do. I'll not be piling more problems on her old shoulders."

"Damn it, Linc, you're acting like a child."

Since Linc couldn't use either hand or elbow, it took some doing for him to lever himself off the mattress, but he finally managed to sit up and glare hotly at his cousin. "All right, you cocky bastard. If you think—"

"Stop it! Stop it right now!" Victoria shouted at the two men. "There's no need for all this arguing."

"You're damn right, there's not," Ross said flatly. "Linc is going to do what I say!"

"Like hell!" Linc muttered.

Victoria interceded once again. "That's enough. Nobody is going to make Linc do something he doesn't want to do," she said to Ross and then resting her hands on the footboard of the bed, she leaned toward Linc and smiled encouragingly. "I have the solution, Linc. Your parents' old house is empty. Grady, the foreman on the fence-building crew moved out a week ago. He bought a place of his own. So we'll have the house clean and ready for you by tomorrow."

Relief washed over Linc's face. "Victoria, you're a real darlin'."

"My husband tells me that very same thing everyday," she teased, then walked to the head of the bed, where she bent down and placed a kiss on Linc's clammy forehead. "Don't worry, cuz, I'm not going to let anyone badger you. Especially my mean ol' brother."

"Aw, Victoria, quit babying the man," Ross complained, but there was a half grin on his face to soften his words. "You'll have him so spoiled by the time he gets well, he'll be worthless to all of us."

This time Linc didn't let Ross's jabs rile him. Now that he knew where he was going to go once he was released from the hospital, there was another pressing problem on his mind.

"Sounds good, Victoria, but what about a nurse? I can't imagine any woman wanting to stay out at the ranch. Especially not round the clock."

Victoria frowned at him. "Why not? The ranch is beautiful. And even though the house isn't anything fancy, it's very nice."

Linc shrugged as memories of his mother pushed at the edges of his thoughts. Darla had hated the ranch. The dust, the livestock, the isolation and the constant work it took from her husband to make the place go. He could still remember her arguing fiercely with his father and constantly throwing in his face threats to leave him and the whole mess behind.

Eventually his mother *had* left the ranch. But not until his father had died from the heart disease that had slowly debilitated him. Linc had been a young teenager when his father had finally passed away and at the time he'd often wondered why Darla bothered to hang around. She'd obviously not given a hoot for her husband. And she had not shown much more concern for Linc. She'd been content to let him run loose on the ranch and more or less take care of himself.

Darla had remarried quickly after his father's death and to his amazement, she'd demanded that Linc move to the east coast with her and her new husband. If the idea hadn't been so ludicrous it would have been laughable. Linc had lived his whole life on the T Bar K. He'd grown up with cousins who were his own age. The place was his home and would always be his home. He wasn't about to move to some city, away from everything he loved. So he'd chosen to stay behind and his mother had walked away without a backward glance.

"Well, yeah," he finally said to Victoria. "But some women—"

"I'm not going to hire just some woman," Victoria assured him. "If she isn't nice and reasonable, dedicated and completely qualified, then she isn't going to step foot on the ranch. Understand?"

Linc wanted to tell her that there wasn't any such woman of that sort who'd be willing to live under the same roof with him, even in a nurse/patient situation. But he kept his mouth shut. He'd already done enough arguing and complaining and Victoria was doing the best she could. At the very least, he was grateful.

"Where are you going to find a woman like that?" Ross questioned his sister. "They don't grow on trees around here, you know."

She made a face at her brother. "I am a doctor, remember? I do have sources. Trust me, I'll find one."

Quickly skirting the bed, Ross looped his arm through Victoria's and tugged her toward the door. "Sounds like a big job to me. You'd better get out of here and get started on it. Linc and I have important things to discuss."

"I hope it's horses," Linc said from his

seat on the bed. "Because I'm sure sick of discussing nurses!"

"Oh, all right, I'm out of here," Victoria said with a helpless shake of her head. "But just remember, Linc, you can't get back to work until you heal. And you'll need a nurse to get you there."

"Yeah. Well, I guess a man can stand most anything if he has to," Linc muttered.

LATER THAT AFTERNOON, Nevada Ortiz was in the middle of trying to immunize a baby boy, who was displaying a whale of a screaming fit, when her boss, Dr. Victoria Hastings called to her.

"Nevada, as soon as you're finished there, I want to see you in my office."

Nevada swiped the baby's thigh with an alcohol square and tried to still his kicking foot.

"What about Mr. Buckhorn?" Nevada called to her. "He's in the waiting room and Joyce says he already went outside twice to smoke a cigarette."

Clearly frustrated, Victoria let out a sigh.

"All right. I'll finish up with him and then I'll see you in my office."

"She sounds like she means business," the young woman holding the baby said. "What have you done wrong, Nevada?"

Since Aztec, New Mexico, was a small town, almost everyone was acquainted with each other. And since Nevada had worked as a nurse in Aztec for six of her twenty-five years, she'd met lots of people, including the young mother holding squalling Henry.

Nevada shrugged and smiled. "Not too much today. But little Henry may disagree." She rubbed the spot on the baby's thigh where she'd injected him, and after about two seconds his cries were replaced with a dimpled smile. "Now see there," she told the boy, "that wasn't so bad, was it? And look what you get now."

Reaching into her uniform pocket, she pulled out a red lollipop, removed the cellophane and handed the treat to the baby. Grabbing it, he let out a happy coo and Nevada patted his cheek.

"Be sure that you watch him for any signs of fever or rash," she told the mother. "Since this is a booster, I don't expect him to have any problems, but if he does, go ahead and give us a call."

"I will. Thank you, Nevada."

Once she was sure mother and baby were on their way out of the examining room, Nevada hurried to the front of the building to retrieve Mr. Buckhorn's chart from the hundreds that filled the shelves on a wall behind the receptionist's desk.

Leaning down, she whispered in Joyce's ear, "Has he been outside again? Or just having a cussing fit?"

The receptionist didn't have to be told that Nevada was talking about Mr. Buckhorn. He was the only patient left in the waiting room.

"Neither, thank God," the receptionist answered. "I turned the television on to the Western channel. Sunset Carson is keeping him occupied."

Smiling, Nevada picked up the elderly

man's chart and walked to the door of the waiting room. "Mr. Buckhorn, you can come back now," she called to him.

The old Navajo slowly turned his head and leveled an annoyed look at her. "I've already waited too long, young lady." He jabbed a finger in the direction of the television. "I gotta see what this cowboy is gonna do with this gunslinger."

"He's going to shoot him, that's what," Nevada told him. "And Dr. Hastings is going to shoot you if you don't get back here. She doesn't have time to wait around on old men like you."

Mumbling what sounded like Navajo curse words, the old man slapped a beat-up cowboy hat on his head and slowly rose to his feet. By the time he made it to Nevada, though, he was in a better mood and his wide, wrinkled grin made his dark eyes sparkle playfully.

"I'm not so old, missy. I have a girlfriend. See her every day, too."

"Smells like you have a cigarette every

day, too. You know that Doc is gonna be angry with you."

His chuckles were full of mischief. "She'll get over it."

MORE THAN THIRTY minutes later, Nevada was finally able to meet with Victoria. The day had been long and both women were exhausted. Nevada practically fell into the stuffed armchair sitting near the doctor's wide desk.

"What a day!" Nevada exclaimed. "How many patients did we see anyway?"

Victoria tried to smile. "I quit counting after we hit twenty."

Reaching up, Nevada began to pull the pins from the braided black bun at the back of her head. Once the last one was removed, the long silky strands fell to her shoulders, and she gave the heavy mane a shake.

"So, what have I done now?" Nevada asked her boss. "Made a patient angry? I know Mr. Tallman complained about the shot I gave him. But honestly, Victoria, the man is a wimp."

Leaning back in her chair, Victoria chuckled tiredly. "You haven't done a thing wrong, Nevada. And you're right, he is a wimp. But none of that is why I wanted to talk to you this evening."

Nevada looked at her boss with interest. "Oh? What's happened? Are you going to take off work or something?"

Victoria slowly shook her head. "Actually, I probably should take off work. But right now it's just not feasible. Dr. Martinez is out of town on vacation and won't be back for one more week. I have no one to replace me. At least, no one that I would trust with my patients." Folding her hands atop the desk, she leaned up and looked intently at Nevada. "You see, I'm having a problem. I'm hunting a dependable nurse. Someone I can really count on."

Shocked, Nevada stared at the other woman. "Oh. You mean, uh—you think I can't handle all the work around here? I thought you and I worked well together."

Victoria quickly waved a hand at her. "Nevada, my dear, I couldn't do without you. You're my right arm. And I really don't know how I'm going to get through the next few weeks if you agree to this."

"This?" Nevada asked carefully. "What *is* this?"

Massaging her forehead, Victoria said, "I need you to do me a favor. A big favor."

"Of course. Anything," Nevada quickly agreed.

"Wait a minute," Victoria said as her hand fell away from her face. "You'd better hear me out before you agree. This might be a project you won't want to get yourself into."

Nevada scooted onto the edge of her seat. "You've got me curious now. And you know how much I love challenges."

Chuckling, Victoria said, "Well, I have a feeling this will be one. You know my cousin Linc was burned badly in the barn fire at the ranch."

Nevada nodded soberly. "Yes. How is he doing?"

"Actually, he's going to be released from the hospital tomorrow."

Nevada shot her boss a bright smile. "That's good news. From what you told me, his burns were very serious. He must be doing much better."

"He is. And Ross and I persuaded the doctor that he'd do even better if he was allowed to go home. The doctor agreed. But only if we could find a nurse to stay with him round the clock. I thought of you."

"Me!" Nevada's hand fluttered to her chest. "Victoria! I—I couldn't."

Victoria leveled a wry look at her. "You just told me you would do anything."

"Yes, I did. But I didn't have any idea you'd be asking something like this. I don't even know your cousin! And I'd practically be living with the man!"

"You *would* be living with him," Victoria corrected. "He can't be left alone. He can't use his hands in any way. Not yet. So you can imagine how much care he's going to need."

"Yes, I can imagine." Nevada felt awful

for Linc Ketchum. Even though she'd never met the man, she understood the pain and suffering he must be going through. She'd attended to many burn patients over her years of nursing and she understood the care he would need. But she didn't really want to leave her home for two or three weeks. And living with a man? Well, she'd always been adventurous but that was taking it a bit too far.

"But I really don't think I'm the nurse you need."

"You're exactly the nurse Linc needs. These injuries haven't just disabled him physically, they've tugged him down emotionally. Normally, Linc is a gentle, easy-going man. Everyone admires and loves him. But this morning he actually cussed at Ross. He needs to get his mind off the fire and off his confinement. If anyone can do that, you can."

Nevada let out an incredulous laugh. "How? By playing dominos or poker with the man? Victoria, I don't know anything about him. I wouldn't even know how to talk to him."

Smiling, Victoria said, "You? Not know how to talk to a man? Come on, my dear, that sort of thing comes to you naturally."

"That's another thing. I have a life here in town. How could I go out on dates if I'm stuck on the T Bar K? You know that I have boyfriends. They won't understand."

"If that's the case, you don't need them."

A long sigh slipped past Nevada's lips. She'd tried, but she could see there was no talking Victoria out of this. "You really mean this, don't you?"

"Nevada. I can't think of anyone better," she said with a soft voice. "No one else would suit Linc. He's a man who needs gentle care."

Nevada studied Victoria's face and could easily see the signs of worry etching her eyes and mouth. "You love your cousin very much, don't you?"

Victoria nodded. "I always have. Linc is special—to all of us. He's like our brother. And yet he's always wanted to remain independent. I don't know why. But he's a strong, compassionate man and it makes me want to sob when I see him like he is now."

Feeling her eyes grow misty, Nevada walked around the desk and placed a hand on Victoria's slender shoulder. "Don't worry. You should know I'll take on the job. I can't say no to you even when I want to."

Victoria looked up at her gratefully. "Don't do this just for me, Nevada. Do it for Linc. Okay?"

Uneasiness rippled through Nevada and made her hesitate. But only for a moment and then she smiled. "All right. I'll do this for Linc."

Chapter Two

He was sitting on the porch of his father's old house when a little white sports car covered with the red dust of T Bar K land pulled to a stop a few feet from the rail fence that enclosed the house and yard, a yard which was little more than a patch of raw mountain land filled with boulders, pine trees and sagebrush.

Rising slowly from his chair, Linc ambled toward the fence as his squinted eyes tried to make out the person behind the dusty windshield. And as he waited for the nurse to climb out of the vehicle he told himself it didn't matter what sort of person this woman was just so long as she stayed out of his hair as much as possible.

The door to the car finally swung open

and Linc caught the glimpse of jeans-clad legs and long, raven-black hair being blown by the evening breeze.

He watched her catch her flyaway hair with a brown hand as she turned to greet him.

"Hello," she called cheerfully. "I guess you must be Linc."

Dear God, what had Victoria done to him, he wondered. This woman wasn't a nurse. She couldn't be. She was very young and looked more like a sexy siren than a caregiver. Her petite body had more curves than the mountain road leading up to the house and her face was full of dimples, sparkling brown eyes and lips the color of a ripe cherry. This was not the sort of woman he needed sleeping across the hall from him.

"That would be me," he replied, while wondering how he could tell her to go home and still be polite about it.

She walked up to him and smiled. "I'd offer you my hand. But since you can't take it, I'll just say I'm glad to be here."

Topping her jeans was a red jersey shirt that had slipped down on one shoulder. On her small feet were wedge sandals tall enough to break her ankles. Linc couldn't prevent his gaze from climbing up from her painted toenails to the top of her head and back down again. "Where did Victoria find you?" he asked rudely.

The blunt question lifted Victoria's delicate black brows. "Well, not out of a hole if that's what you're thinking. I'm her nurse. I figured you knew that. Haven't you ever been to Victoria's clinic?"

He shook his head while hating the fact that she was making him feel downright stupid. "I don't ever need to be doctored." He frowned as his gaze focused on his bandaged hands. "At least, not until the fire."

"Well, you must be very lucky," Nevada said while her eyes took in the sight of Victoria's cousin.

He practically glowered at her and lifted the thick white bandages directly in front of her face.

"Lucky? You call this lucky?"

Unaffected by his sarcasm, she nodded. "If you've lived all these years without needing a doctor's care, you're a very fortunate man, Linc Ketchum. And as for those—" she inclined her head toward his burns, "better your hands than your whole body being toasted."

She was right and he knew it, but that didn't make him feel any better. Still, he thanked God that he'd gotten out of the fire before it had consumed him.

"Yeah," he said, then walking around her, he peered into the car's back seat. It was piled with enough luggage to fill two closets. His jaw tightened. "It looks like you've come to stay."

Turning slightly toward him, Nevada frowned. "Of course I've come to stay. You need someone here with you at all times."

He drew in a bracing breath then blew it out. "Well, I don't want to sound rude, but I don't think you're gonna be that person."

She whirled completely around to stare at him. "What?"

He shrugged as a sheepish expression

stole over his lean face. Normally he went to great lengths to handle people gently, the same way he handled his horses. But this firebrand standing in front of him was scratching his hackles in the wrong direction.

"I said I don't think you're the right person to stay with me."

Nevada's eyes narrowed as her hands came to rest on either side of her waist. "You don't, huh? Well, just what sort of person would you like to have staying with you?" she asked in a voice that dripped sweetness.

"None! Damn it. I can get along without anybody's help. And I have no idea why Victoria sent you up here! I don't even believe you're a nurse!"

Nevada folded her arms against her breasts. This outburst from her patient wasn't too big a surprise. Victoria had already warned her that since the fire Linc had been on a rampage. And she'd heard a long time ago that the man was a recluse. She'd asked Victoria about the hearsay and the doctor had confirmed it as true, saying she couldn't remember the last time Linc Ketchum had ever stepped foot off the T Bar K. Poor man, Nevada thought. He really needed her help.

"Why not?" she asked simply.

He stepped closer and it was then that Nevada allowed herself to really look at him. When she'd first driven up, she'd gotten the impression of long legs, muscles and shoulders broad enough to carry her weight twice over. Now she could study his face close up and as far as she was concerned it was a work of pure art.

A Roman nose, square jaw and chin, and dark-green eyes set beneath a pair of black brows. At the moment he was wearing a cowboy hat the color of creamed coffee, but she could see the hair next to it was slightly darker and curled against his head in a touch-me-please way. Victoria had told her that Linc was thirty-eight and all Nevada could think at the moment was what a hunk of a man Linc Ketchum had grown into in those thirty-eight years.

"Because you don't look like a nurse. Or sound like one, either," he answered.

Nevada couldn't help but laugh. "Really? I guess you must be an expert on nurses?"

He grimaced. "No. But—"

Nevada stepped forward and put her hand on his shoulder. It was warm, rock-hard and caused her skin to sizzle.

"Listen, Linc. Victoria tried to find a nurse other than me. She couldn't. No one was willing to come all the way out here and stay for two weeks."

"That's not surprising," Linc muttered. "If a woman has to go without electricity for one hour, she thinks she's been traumatized."

"Hmm. Is that so? I had to go without electricity for two days last winter. Ice did something to the lines going to my apartment. But you know, I made it okay. Didn't feel a bit traumatized."

Glowering, he looked away from her. "I guess you're trying to say that I should be grateful that you were willing to take care of me?"

Her hand felt as though it was vibrating on his shoulder and she pulled it away, hoping it would put an end to the odd sensation. "Well, you don't have to go so far as to be grateful. Just civil will be enough for me."

His head twisted back around and Nevada felt something jerk in her chest as his dark-green gaze landed on her face. "You're doing this for Victoria's sake, aren't you?" he asked, then quickly added, "No. Don't answer that. I already know that you are."

"Well, well. You not only think you're an expert on nurses, you also think you're a mind reader. You must have many talents, Mr. Ketchum."

Ignoring her sarcasm, he said, "See, you're not even bothering to deny it."

Nevada smiled at him. "Why should I bother? You seem to know the answer already."

He heaved out a heavy breath. "Well, I guess that part of it doesn't matter. I just don't like feeling beholden to anybody."

Nevada's expression turned serious.

"Look, Linc, I'm here because I chose to be here. I'm a nurse and when it all boils down, I can't turn away from someone who needs my help. No matter who they're related to. Now if you don't mind, I need to unload my things from the car."

She stepped around him and jerked the car door open. Linc watched with helpless frustration as she pulled out several pieces of luggage and piled them on the ground. Normally, he would never allow a female to lift anything heavier than a plate of food in his presence. But as it was he was so incapacitated he couldn't even pick up her handbag.

"If you need help with that I can call someone up from the main house," he finally offered.

She glanced his way. "Thank you. But they're not a problem for me to carry."

He watched her shove one of the bags beneath her armpit and pick up two more with her hands. How the hell was he going to deal with this woman for two weeks or more, he wondered. She'd already managed to make him feel like a helpless idiot. Moreover, she was just too damn sexy.

"I—uh—I'd help if I could," he felt compelled to say.

She started moving toward the house and he fell in beside her.

"I know that," she said. "Don't apologize for your condition. You can't help it. Just try to get well as quickly as you can."

The two of them crossed the rough ground of the yard and climbed onto the porch. There Nevada turned to look at the view. The house was facing south and some distance over on the next mountain ridge she could spot the top of the main ranch house. Between here and there was nothing but forested mountains.

"This is beautiful," she said with quiet awe.

Linc looked at her, faintly surprised by the sincerity in her voice. "Yeah, but give yourself a few days and you'll be screaming to see town again."

She flashed him a glance. "How could you predict that? You don't even know me."

"Women can't stand the isolation."

Obviously Linc Ketchum wasn't just down on being incapacitated, he was also down on women for some reason that Nevada would very much like to know.

"Excuse me, but Victoria lived her whole life on this ranch until she went to med school and married Jess."

He waved away her words. "Victoria is different. She's a ranch girl, a cowgirl."

Nevada wanted to ask him what he thought she was, but she didn't bother. Now wasn't the time to try to dig into him. If she was going to be able to make it through the next two or three weeks, she needed to keep peace with the man.

"Well, don't worry about me getting cabin fever. I'm sure you'll keep me entertained," she said, then turning to the door, she opened it and stepped inside.

Linc quickly followed her into the small foyer and then into the long living room until she stopped abruptly and stared all around her.

"Oh! This is lovely. This looks almost like the big ranch house. Only smaller."

The room had off-white walls and a high ceiling crossed with heavy oak beams stained a deep brown. The floor was covered with a shiny brown-and-beige tile and a good portion of the north wall was built of plate glass. The landscape past the window was breathtaking and framed the peaks of the distant San Juan Mountains, which, in spite of it being midsummer, still hung on to their caps of snow.

"You sound surprised," Linc said as he watched her drop her bags and walk slowly around the room. "What were you expecting?"

She shot him a frank glance. "Nothing like this. Victoria told me this was just a small ranch house that they leased to any of the ranch hands who had a family and were in need of housing."

"She told you right."

"Goodness! This is so—beautiful!" Continuing her walk around the room, she inspected the leather furniture, the Western photos and paintings on the walls and the wagon wheel that dropped from the center beam in the ceiling. The wooden wheel was circled with lights that were fashioned in the shape of old-time lanterns.

The fact that she was so taken with the house both surprised and pleased Linc. He hadn't expected such a reaction from her. To look at her, she seemed like the modern-apartment type.

"I'm sure it seems dated and stuffy to you."

"Not at all," she said as she headed toward an opening that looked as though it would lead to the kitchen area.

Linc followed her into the kitchen to a pine table and benches located near another wide window. From here Nevada could look down upon the ranch. From this angle, looking left, she could see a meadow filled with black Angus cattle and the sparkling ribbon that was the Animas River.

"Where do you live?" Linc wanted to know.

She glanced away from the window and

over to him. He was standing only a couple of feet away from her and she picked up the faint masculine scent of his body. An inward shiver raced through her as she looked at him, and she hoped the reaction wasn't showing on her face. The last thing she needed was for this man to think she was attracted to him.

Which she wasn't. She couldn't be. He was a patient.

"In Aztec. In an apartment." She grinned wryly. "My kitchen view is of an alleyway. The only good thing about it is that I get to see an assortment of stray cats hunting through the garbage cans."

"Hmmph. I'll bet you're the kind of woman who pours feed out for them."

She laughed guiltily. "Well, I am soft-hearted when it comes to animals," she admitted. "And I'd never let one go hungry for any reason."

"You like animals?" he asked.

Once again he sounded surprised and Nevada wondered where he'd formed his opinions about women.

"Very much. In fact when I first started college I had plans to become a veterinarian. But then a close friend of mine became seriously ill and I decided that maybe I was meant to help people get well."

"Did you help your friend?"

Shaking her head, Nevada turned away from him. He didn't need to see any sort of sadness or woe on her face. Not now. Linc Ketchum needed to see bright skies ahead and she was determined to show them to him. "No. She died. And that only reinforced my resolve to stay in medicine." Turning she smiled at him. "But that's in the past. And right now I think I'd better go carry in the rest of my things and get settled in."

She turned and walked out of the kitchen and Linc found himself wanting to follow her, talk to her, if for no other reason than to hear her voice. Which didn't make one iota of sense to him.

Linc didn't talk to women just for the sake of making conversation. Sure there were women who came to the T Bar K

looking to buy a horse or colt or have a
mare bred by one of the ranch's champion
stallions. And Linc didn't have any problems dealing with them. But as far as his
personal life went, he'd always made it a
policy to steer clear of women.

It wasn't that he disliked the opposite
sex. To Linc, women were pretty much like
the horses he tended. Most of them were
very beautiful, but they were also high-
strung and unpredictable. If he ever let his
guard down around one, even the sweet-na-
tured ones, he was taking a big risk of getting hurt, and hurt badly. So he stayed alert
and safe around his horses and the women
he happened to come in contact with.

The front door opened and closed for a
second time and he realized Nevada had
already returned to the house. He quickly
left the kitchen and walked out to the living
room to see her hefting three more bags.

"If you'll show me where I'll be sleeping, I'll get these things out of the way,"
she told him.

As he walked across the long room to

join her, he thought about having her sleep in the small upstairs bedroom. The farther he could put her away from him, the better he'd feel. And the room did have a pretty view and a nice set of oak bedroom furniture. But it would be mean of him to make her climb the stairs with all those things. So he motioned for her to follow him down a long wide hall that was covered with more tile.

Halfway down the corridor, he motioned to their left. "There's two rooms here that are pretty much the same. Take your pick. It doesn't matter to me," he lied.

Her gaze went from one door to the other, then across the hall to where two more doors were located. "Where is your room?" she asked.

Frowning, he asked, "Is that really important?"

She made a face of disbelief. "You *are* my patient. I need to be as close as possible. It will make things easier for me and you both."

"I don't need help getting to bed."

Dropping the bags, she turned a disgusted look on him. "Really? You can unbutton your jeans and shirt? You can pull back the covers?"

Dear Lord, he was going crazy. Of course he couldn't do those things. But how in hell could he let this woman undress him? To have her pretty brown hands touching him in such a way would be downright decadent.

"Well, I can manage somehow. There's no need—"

"Look, Linc Ketchum, this is no time to be bashful or modest. I'm a nurse. I know all about men's anatomies. Helping you out of your jeans won't turn me three shades of red or make me want to attack you with lust in my eyes."

She was so cute and sassy and reasonable that it made him furious. But he tried his best to bite it all back and behave as the cool cowboy he'd always believed himself to be.

"Miss Ortiz, you've just relieved all my worries," he said curtly.

She studied his face, the faint grin on her lips coming and going along with the dimples in her cheeks. Linc forced himself to stay put even though her nearness was affecting him the way the scent of a wild deer excites a docile horse.

"I'm glad we got all that straight," she said. "It would be awkward if we rubbed each other the wrong way right from the start."

As far as Linc was concerned it would be awkward if they rubbed each other any way. But then he couldn't rub her even if he wanted to. Not with hands that resembled two white clubs.

Trying not to look petulant, he jerked his head toward the door behind him. "That's my room. So this one—" he motioned to the door behind her shoulder. "Would be the closest to mine."

"Okay."

She turned and opened the door and Linc felt compelled to follow her into the bedroom.

"Oh! This is lovely, too. Goodness, Victoria must have sent an army of maids up here. Everything looks so beautiful and it smells like wood polish."

She walked over and trailed her fingers over the fat carved end post of the bed. Linc was surprised that she was so impressed with the house and its furnishings. He expected that as a nurse she made a very nice salary. Victoria wanted the best in her clinic, and he knew she would be willing to pay far more than hospital wages to this woman. But apparently she wasn't used to expensive surroundings.

"Then I take it that the room is okay with you?" he asked.

She glanced around the room which had a small alcove that held a desk, chair and a graceful floor lamp.

"It's more than okay. It's just great," she murmured as she ran fingers along the silky comforter on the bed. Turning to him, she smiled. "I've never lived anywhere this nice before. I'm not going to know how to feel," she said, then laughing, she bounced on the edge of the mattress. "No broken springs or sags in the middle."

"I'm sure your apartment is very nice," he said as he stood watching her playful antics and wondering how it must feel to be that young and carefree. It had been so long, years and years, since he'd raced over the ranch yard with Ross and Seth and yelled at the top of his lungs with the pure joy of being alive and happy.

Seeing the sober look on his face took away some of the pleasure Nevada was feeling and the smile faded from her face. "It is nice for what I can afford. It takes a lot of money for rent and everything else that goes with making a living. Especially when you're trying to save, too."

Linc suddenly felt a little ashamed of himself. He'd never had to worry about money. His father had left him a fairly large inheritance and since then he'd earned plenty by managing the horse-breeding program for the ranch. In fact, money was something Linc rarely thought about. His home was on the ranch and he didn't want for many material things. But apparently Nevada didn't have it so easy.

"What are you saving for?"

She appeared surprised that he asked the question and frankly, he'd surprised himself. It was none of his business what she did with herself or her money. But something seemed to have happened to his common sense since Nevada Ortiz stepped out of her dusty little car.

She shrugged. "Oh, well, you know, the normal things. Mainly the future. For a family."

His brows slowly lifted as he watched her wavy black hair slide over one pert little breast. "You have someone you're planning to make a family with?"

Laughing softly, she rose from the mattress. "Goodness no! I have plenty of boyfriends, but none of them are husband material."

His frown was tinged with disgust. "If they're not husband material, then what are they?"

"Well, I'm sure you have girlfriends. It's

the same thing. They're just companions, guys that I enjoy doing things with."

Linc wanted to kick himself for suddenly feeling so disillusioned. Just what was he expecting from this woman? he asked himself. She was young and beautiful. No doubt she had plenty of men friends she enjoyed herself with. To her they were probably nothing more than toys.

Ignoring the part about the girlfriends, he said, "If that's the case, then what do you call husband material?"

Pursing her lips with displeasure she shook her head. "I'm not really thinking about that now. I'm only twenty-five. I'm not ready to settle down. In fact, I'm not sure that I ever want to get married."

"You just said you wanted a family," he reminded her.

Her expression went stone-sober as she walked past him and picked up one of the cases she'd left in the doorway.

"I do. I just can't figure out how to have one without having a man in the house with me. Unfortunately you need one to produce children." Sighing, she placed the duffel bag upon the bed and began to pull out a stack of blue jeans. "But I keep hoping that someday I'll meet a man who will change my mind about love."

Love. Now that was a word he never spoke, didn't believe in, or want it discussed in his presence. It made him feel very squeamish.

Realizing it was long past time he left the room, Linc turned toward the door only to have her call after him.

"Where are you going?"

Without looking at her, he said, "To call down to the ranch to see if they can round you up a television from the big house. You're going to need something to keep you busy."

Her tinkling laugh filled the bedroom. "I don't need a television. I've got you to keep me busy."

Like hell, Linc thought.

Chapter Three

More than an hour passed before Nevada finished unpacking her things and arranging them just as she wanted in the big bedroom. The dresser and chest were massive, along with the walk-in closet. She could have brought every piece of clothing and toiletries she owned and they wouldn't have filled half the available space.

Nevada couldn't believe the house had been built just for the sole purpose of extra housing for ranch workers. It was too beautiful and, in spite of its old age, had been kept in perfect condition. Someone had taken great pains to copy the big ranch house and rich details could be seen in the dark oak casings around the windows and doors, the expensive tiling on the floor, not to mention the nice furnishings.

The first moment she'd walked into the house, she'd felt some sort of strange connection, a feeling that made her wonder if she was experiencing what it felt like to go home. Which had been an odd reaction for Nevada. Since she'd been a very young child, she hadn't ever felt like she had a home. At least, not like regular folks.

Even though she'd grown up in a house with two parents, it had been far from a normal home. Her mother and father had quarreled incessantly until their arguments had become out-and-out fights that included throwing fists and objects. Nevada had often hidden in the closet praying for the noise to stop and praying, too, that she would someday be able to escape the house that seemed to be filled with nothing but hate.

No. Nevada wasn't exactly sure what a real home would feel like, but she was certain this old house might hold the answers.

Giving one last look over her shoulder,

she left the room. Her medical bag was still in the car and she wanted to get Linc's bandages changed before it was time for dinner. Something she was to cook, she supposed, since the closest restaurants or delis were at least twenty miles away. Nevada wasn't exactly brilliant in the kitchen, but if necessary she could put something edible on the table.

Humming to herself, she stepped onto the porch and immediately spotted Linc sitting a few steps away in a wooden rocker. His felt hat was pulled down over his eyes, but the moment he heard her footsteps and the creaking of the screen door closing behind her, he pushed it back on his forehead and cocked an eye at her.

"What are you doing?"

The question seemed comical to her and she laughed softly. "Does it matter?"

He scooted up from his slumped position in the chair. "No. Since you're going to be here for a while, I can't start worrying whether you can take care of yourself or not."

She walked over to him. "What do you mean, take care of myself?"

He shrugged one thick shoulder. "I just meant you surely have enough sense not to do silly things. Like walk out in the woods by yourself."

Nevada frowned. "Why shouldn't I walk in the woods?"

He let out a long sigh. "Bears for one thing. Another, you'd turn around once and be lost. The mountains and the basins begin to all look the same. You'd probably be to the Colorado border before you realized you were going north."

Nevada had to admit she wasn't necessarily good with directions and as for bears, one of those hairy creatures was the last thing she wanted to meet up with.

Smiling at him, she said, "You're probably right about that. I have to take a map with me just to find my way around Santa Fe. But that doesn't mean I can't get out in the woods. You'll be along to help me find the way."

Linc's mouth fell open. "Bullsh—"

He stopped abruptly before he released the last of the curse word and Nevada only smiled wider.

"What's the matter now? You don't like to take walks?" she asked.

Linc rolled his eyes. "I use my legs for a purpose. I walk all over the ranch yard. I don't walk for a woman's entertainment."

"But you're not working down at the ranch yard now," she sweetly pointed out. "And if it's safe to ask, just what do you do to entertain a woman? Can you sing or play the guitar?"

He scowled. "No and no."

"Oh," she said with feigned disappointment. "I thought all cowboys could do those two things."

"Only on television," he grumbled.

"Well, I'm sure you have some talents. And I'm bound to discover what they are before I leave here."

"Don't bet on that."

Laughing softly, Nevada stepped off the porch and walked to her car. Once she had the medical bag out of the trunk, she carried it to the porch and motioned for Linc to follow her inside.

"What do you have there?" he asked suspiciously without making a move to do her bidding.

"My medical bag. And there's not a thing in here that will hurt you. So get to your feet and come along."

"I don't need any medicine. I've already taken it for today," he said as he managed to rise to his feet without the help of his arms or hands.

The man must have rock-hard abs, Nevada thought, to raise himself up with no help from his upper limbs. But she didn't need to be thinking about Linc Ketchum's abs or the whipcord strength of his body. She was here to nurse, not daydream.

"I'm not going to give you any medicine," she assured him, then shot him a little smile that was a bit wicked. "I have other things I need to do to you."

Eying her through narrowed lashes, Linc stopped in his tracks. "Whoa now," he said firmly. "If you think I'm going to blindly follow your orders, you're crazy, woman."

Nevada lifted her gaze to the ceiling of the porch and hummed a bit of a song about suspicious minds.

Linc cursed under his breath. "I'm not suspicious. I just want to know what's going on. It's my body after all," he practically barked.

Compassion filled Nevada's soft heart and with a smile she walked over to him and put her hand on his shoulder. "I'm sorry, Linc. I was only teasing you a little. It's a proven fact that patients get well much faster if they laugh. You really need to loosen up and let loose with a few chuckles."

"I don't have anything to laugh about," he grumbled.

Nevada tugged on his arm and urged him toward the door. "Of course you do. You can laugh at me. I won't mind at all. Besides, I have a nice surprise for you."

As Linc allowed her to lead him into the house and then the kitchen, he didn't question her further. He was too busy noticing how it felt to have her arm wrapped around his, her hip and thigh softly brushing against him.

He couldn't remember the last time he'd touched a woman. Apparently he'd allowed too much time to pass since he'd gone on the prowl for a little female companionship. Otherwise, he wouldn't be having such a strong reaction to Nevada Ortiz. Sexual starvation could be the only reason he was suddenly noticing the scent of her hair and wondering what she looked like beneath her clothes.

The two of them entered the kitchen and she pointed to the table. "Okay, sit down there while I get everything ready."

Since he was in such a vulnerable condition, it was obvious he was going to have to trust this woman completely. And if Victoria thought so highly of her, she must be a good nurse, Linc told himself. But she didn't look or act like any nurse he'd ever known. And he didn't feel like any normal patient would feel whenever she touched him. But that was something he was going to have to get over. And fast.

With that resolution in his head, he eased down on the long bench and rested his bandaged arms and hands on the table. Like a colorful bird flitting happily from one limb to the next, she moved around the kitchen gathering scissors, towels, tape and a bowl of yellow goop that looked like the sulfur poultices he sometimes used on his horses' cuts and wounds.

"Before I headed out here today," she said as she sat down next to him, "I went by Dr. Olstead's office to pick up my orders for you. He says it's time for you to see that you still have fingers."

Linc's expression was a bit confused. "I've seen my fingers since they were burned. I know that they're still there."

"Yes. But this is going to last for more than just a few minutes," she said, then smiled broadly at his perplexed expression. "Just wait and see."

She picked up a pair of the small scissors that she'd pulled from the medical bag and began to cut through the bandage on his right arm. The white gauze was thickly wrapped and the instrument chewed slowly as Nevada guided it through the material.

While she carefully worked over his arm, Linc studied the shiny crown of her black hair and the dark crescent of long lashes shadowing her cheeks. There wasn't anything about the woman that wasn't fresh and young and lovely. Everything about her glowed like a star plucked from a night sky.

"You like being a nurse?" he asked in hopes that a little conversation would take his mind to more normal things.

"Very much," she answered. "I like helping people."

"Is your mother a nurse?"

His question must have surprised her because she looked up from her task and frowned.

"Heavens no. Mom would run off screaming if she had to change a bandage or a bedpan."

"What does she do?"

Nevada's gaze slipped back to the job of

cutting through the bandage and then she shrugged. "She works as a barmaid. In a tavern over in Bloomfield."

"Oh."

He didn't think there had been any note of disgust in his one word, but she must have thought so. She looked up again and this time her lips were set in a grim line.

"Yeah. Oh. Her job is not something I approve of. But she seems to like it. She says the tips are good." With a heavy sigh, she went back to cutting the last of the gauze away from his arm. "Believe me, Linc, my mother wasn't always—well, let's just say in the past years she's allowed her standards to fall."

Linc didn't know why he'd even questioned her about her mother. He'd thought that maybe she'd gotten her personality from the woman. But apparently mother and daughter weren't on the same wavelength.

"Why is that?"

She kept her gaze focused on her job. "She became—well, I guess you could call it disillusioned with a lot of things. She just gave up on ever having any sort of decent life. You know, a husband, a home, a good job."

"Your parents are divorced?"

She nodded. "For a long time now. Dad liked women. I couldn't count all the affairs he had before the two of them finally ended their marriage."

Linc started to ask her if that was why she hadn't yet married. But he stopped himself. He didn't talk about marriage with any woman. Even in a passing way. And he certainly didn't want this glamour girl to think he had any sort of matrimonial thoughts in his mind.

"That's too bad," was all he could say.

"Yes. Very bad," she said in a resigned voice. "Because of my dad, my mother stopped taking care of herself. She began having affairs just to spite him. And after that everything went downhill."

She looked up at him and he could see shame and sadness in her brown eyes. "I don't really know why I told you all that.

It's not something I go around discussing with anyone."

"I never repeat things told to me in confidence," he said, just in case she was worrying he would tell others about her family.

Shaking her head, she said, "I wasn't worried that you would. It's just not something I talk about."

Linc understood what she meant. Darla, his own mother, was never discussed by him or his cousins. Years ago, her name was brought up from time to time, but now there didn't seem any point to it. None of them really knew if the woman was still alive. And apparently she didn't care enough to let them know.

He noticed Nevada was beginning to peel away the layers of gauze away from his arm and he was relieved by the distraction. He didn't want to think about mothers or parents or ruined marriages. All of which were very unpleasant subjects to Linc.

"Good lord, that arm looks like the skin of a baby mouse," Linc exclaimed as she pulled the gauze completely away from his arm and then carefully rested his elbow on a clean towel.

"That's good. It's pink. It means it's alive and getting good blood flow."

It should be getting plenty of blood flow, Linc thought grimly. Each time the woman got near him he could feel his heart thump into overdrive. A silly reaction and one he'd certainly never experienced before.

He glanced down at his arm and tried not to feel deflated. The new skin was so thin it was practically transparent. All the hair was gone and in places he could see blue blood veins running just below the surface.

"I guess it is healing," he had to concede.

"It is and very nicely, too. That's the way we want to keep things going." With her hand on his upper arm, she carefully twisted his arm back and forth so that she could inspect the top and underneath. "Boy, you really did a number on this one. Is the other arm like this one?" she asked.

"Pretty much."

She glanced up at him and he could feel

the touch of her brown eyes as it slipped all over his face.

"Victoria tells me that you were a hero. She said if it hadn't been for you several of the horses would have burned to death."

He grimaced. "Victoria is biased. She thinks of herself as my sister. She'd never say anything bad about me."

Nevada shot him a faint smile. "Do you think of yourself as her brother?"

Linc had never had such a question put to him and for a moment it took him aback. All these years he'd thought of himself as the cousin, the one standing just on the outside. And it wasn't because Ross or Seth or Victoria had tried to make him feel that way. In reality it had been quite the opposite. Tucker's children had treated him as though he'd been one of Tucker's offspring, too. But there was no escaping facts. He wasn't one of them. And yet he loved them just as much or more than if they had truly been his siblings.

"Yeah. I guess I do," he murmured.

"I'm glad. Because she thinks you're just about the next best thing to pajamas."

Glancing away from her, he said, "I didn't do anything special. Anyone would have gone in after those horses. I just happened to be the first one at the barn."

That wasn't the way Nevada had heard it. Victoria had told her that several of the ranch hands had been at the barn and they'd tried to hold Linc and keep him from running back into the burning building. They had not been able to stop him, and by the time Linc had emerged from the flames, the entire group had begun to think he was dead.

"Well, I'm sure your horses are happy about it. But I'll bet they miss you."

"Dr. Olstead won't let me go near them. Bacteria, he reasons," Linc muttered. "Hell, they're cleaner than I am. The stalled ones get a bath every day."

Nevada smiled with understanding. "Dr. Olstead is right. You don't want to risk getting any sort of infection. It's not that he thinks the horses are unclean, but there's other things around a barn that might harbor bacteria. Like flies and things like that."

"Yeah. I understand. But that doesn't mean I have to like it."

"No. You don't have to like it," she agreed.

Reaching for the scissors, she began to cut away the bandages on his hands. This task took longer, but Linc didn't mind. In spite of all his protests it was more than nice to have this lovely woman touching him so gently, touching him as though she really cared about his health and well being.

Don't start thinking along those lines, Linc. Just because a woman acts sweet and gentle on the outside doesn't mean she's all goodness on the inside.

His hands had been burned even worse than his arms and Nevada clicked her tongue with misgivings as she unwrapped each finger. "God, this must have been painful. Does any of it still hurt you?" she asked. "If it does, just let me know. I have painkillers in my bag."

"No. None of it hurts. In fact, it mostly doesn't have any feeling at all," he told her. "If I touched your arm, I doubt I'd feel it." At least not in his fingertips, Linc thought. But the rest of his body darn sure would.

She nodded soberly. "The nerve endings in your skin were burned."

"Will it always be that way?"

Her brows pulled together as she gave her head a little shake. "I'm not sure about that, Linc. I think that problem will get better in time, but I can't make you any promises. I'm just an RN not a doctor."

She proceeded to clean his hand and arm and then slather it with the yellow goo. Once she had every spot of his limb covered with the stuff, she began to wind clean gauze around his arm.

"I guess there'll be plenty of scars once the skin heals," he mused aloud. "What about the hair on my forearms? Will it ever come back?"

She looked up at him and gently smiled. "I'm not totally certain about that either. I'd say probably. At least part of it. But who cares whether you have hair on your fore-arms? You can always wear long sleeves. They look more masculine to me, anyway."

He drew in a deep breath and pushed it out. "You have an answer for everything, don't you?"

She shot him an annoyed look, then laughed softly. "Look, Linc, I'm going to be honest with you. A few scars or a lack of hair is nothing to what you could have had. It's a miracle you're alive. So you'd better be thankful."

He glowered at her. "You think I need your preaching to tell me that?"

"You haven't heard preaching from me—yet," she warned.

"Hmmph," he snorted. "For someone so little you're sure full of sass."

"That's to make up for my size," she reasoned pleasantly.

As far as Linc was concerned, he didn't see a thing wrong with her size. Everything was put together perfectly. Too perfectly for his peace of mind.

"Can I wiggle my fingers?" he asked

as he forced himself to focus on anything but her.

She raised up from ministering to his arm. "Sure. Wiggle all you want."

Linc attempted to flex his bare fingers, which still looked like sticks of watermelon to him. "All the time I was in the hospital, I kept thinking how good it would feel to bend my fingers. But it—well," he grimaced as he tried to close them into his fist. "It doesn't feel all that good. They're stiff."

"That will soon change," she promised. "I'm going to bandage each finger lightly so you can move them around and maybe use them just a little. But I mean very little."

He looked at her with surprise. "You mean I don't have to go around with my hands plastered against boards?"

She gave him a happy smile. "Nope. Now, isn't that good news? And aren't you sorry about all this whining and griping?"

The expression that stole over his face was mostly sheepish, but the upward curve of the corner of his lips told her he was definitely pleased.

"Maybe I have been a little cranky," he admitted.

She couldn't help but laugh. "Is that normally your nature?"

He frowned. "Why do you ask that?"

Nevada made a palms up gesture. "Because I don't know you, Linc Ketchum. I don't know if you're usually grouchy or cheerful or sweet or mean or what."

"You're not here to analyze my personality," he reasoned. "And you don't need to know any of those things just to doctor my hands."

Nevada was going to be doing more than doctoring his hands, she wanted to point out, but she didn't say that to him. She could see that it was disturbing to this man to have her here in the house. So far she'd tried to keep everything as light and playful as she could. And she hoped she could keep their time together on that same track. It wouldn't do for both of them to get serious.

"Well, I guess I'll learn for myself," she said as she picked up a roll of gauze and started one end of it around his thumb. "Do you think you can tell me what you like to eat? Or is that a secret, too?"

"You don't need to worry yourself about that either," he told her. "Marina will be bringing up supper from the big house each evening."

This was news to Nevada. Victoria really hadn't had time yesterday to discuss some of the details about her stay here or her duties to Linc. She'd expected to be preparing some sort of meals for him and herself.

"That's nice. But I hope she'll allow me to do breakfast and lunch."

He studied her through drooped lids and for the first time in Nevada's life she felt her whole body react to a man in a purely sexual way. Heat filled her cheeks and she felt as though her whole body was soon going to be glowing like a firefly.

"What does a nurse know about cooking?"

Nevada drew in a bracing breath and told

herself not to look at him. She couldn't look at him if she expected to get her senses back under control.

"Probably about as much as a cowboy does," she muttered.

He caught her off guard by releasing a low chuckle. "You might be surprised at what I know how to do in the kitchen."

Nevada couldn't keep her gaze from latching on to him and the minute it did her stomach did a nervous jump. Was he talking about cooking, she wondered, or something altogether different?

"Really. Then maybe you could teach me a few things," she ventured.

The amusement on his face disappeared like a cloud slipping past the sun and his gaze traveled from her face to her bosom and back again. "I'm sure you've already learned everything there is to know."

Chapter Four

Something about Linc's words struck Nevada hard and deep. And for the next few minutes she didn't say anything as she finished bandaging his fingers then went to work on his left arm to repeat the same process.

She really didn't know why his remark had bothered her so. Maybe it was the note of disgust she'd picked up in his voice or maybe it was the lewd way he'd looked at her. Either way, it didn't matter, she told herself. Linc Ketchum wouldn't be the first person to think she was a promiscuous young woman. Some of her so-called friends had also accused her of sleeping with a long list of boyfriends. But in reality nothing could be further from the truth.

Nevada was a virgin. And so far she hadn't met one man who would make her want to change that fact.

Even so, she wasn't going to explain any of this to Linc Ketchum. Her sexual habits were none of his business. Pure and simple.

LATER THAT EVENING, after she'd finished dressing Linc's burns, Nevada went outside to explore the rugged landscape of the yard. She was at the back of the house enjoying the sight of the far-distant San Juans when she heard the sound of an approaching vehicle.

Carefully picking her way through the rocks and clumps of blooming sage, she skirted the end of the building to see Marina climbing out of an old red pickup truck.

"Marina! Hello!" she called to the housekeeper.

The large Mexican lady with a heavy braid pinned to the back of her head, turned in the direction of Nevada's voice and smiled broadly when she spotted her.

Nevada waved and hurried over to the woman. Without uttering a word of welcome, she hugged Marina tightly. Nevada didn't get to see her old friend that often. Yet somehow from the very first time Victoria had introduced Nevada to the housekeeper, Marina had felt like the mother that Nevada had always wanted.

"It's good to see you," she said in a thick voice.

Marina's broad face was wreathed in smiles as she stepped back and patted Nevada's cheek. "Lord, Lord, you don't know how glad I am to see you, *chica.* You look beautiful. Just what Linc needs."

Nevada scowled at the other woman. "Marina! I'm not up here for eye candy. I'm nursing Linc."

"Hmmph. There's different ways of nursing, you know."

Nevada decided it would be better to let Marina's remark drop completely and she sniffed at the delicious smell of food wafting from the open window of Marina's truck.

"Mmm. Something sure smells good."

Marina stepped back to the truck and opened the door. Inside on the bench seat was a cardboard box draped with a white towel. "Nothing special. Just some smothered steak and vegetables. Oh, and a few sourdough biscuits."

Nevada groaned. "Marina, don't you be bringing stuff like that up here every evening. I'll weigh a ton before I leave here," she admonished in a teasing voice.

"You could use a little more weight on those bones," the housekeeper told Nevada. "Besides, I know how much Linc loves to eat. And he needs good nourishment to get well."

Nevada was about to assure Marina that she'd make sure the man ate right, when the sound of the front door opening caught her attention.

Both women turned their heads to see Linc stepping out onto the porch. He eyed the two women for a moment before he walked over and took a seat in one of the lawn chairs.

Her face filled with deep concern, Marina lowered her head toward Nevada and said in a quiet voice, "I'm very worried about Linc, *chica*."

"You shouldn't be," Nevada stated with confidence. "His arms and hands are coming along very well. It won't be long before he'll be well again and able to work."

Marina shook her head. "That's not what I'm worried about. His body will heal, yes. But his insides, his heart…it's troubled."

Even though the two of them were too far away from Linc for him to catch any of their words, Nevada felt as if he was hearing every syllable that was being uttered about him.

Turning her back to him, Nevada pretended to examine the items in Marina's food box. "Marina, Linc has been through trauma. It's normal for him to be a little down."

The older woman rolled her eyes toward the sky. "Down? *Chica,* he's never acted like this in his life. Linc has always been the quiet, gentle one of the bunch. He's always been kind through and through. But now, he's like a monster!"

Nevada hadn't known Linc before the accident, but she could agree with that last description. The man certainly hadn't come across as kind and gentle since she'd arrived. He clearly didn't trust her abilities as a nurse and he'd practically accused her of being a slut. How much nicer could a man get, she wondered wryly.

Out loud she said, "That's because he probably feels like a monster, Marina. Think about it. He can't do any of the things he loves to do. That would bother you, too. Don't you think?"

Marina's head tilted from one side to the other as she considered Nevada's explanation. "I guess so. But I'm still worried." She lowered her head even closer to Nevada's and whispered, "I haven't told anyone about this, *chica,* but I've been seeing Linc's momma in my dreams. I don't know what she's doing there and it scares me."

A cool shiver raced down Nevada's back. She'd never been a superstitious woman and she had her doubts about anyone *seeing* things that weren't visible to anyone else. But Marina had a bit of a track record for envisioning forthcoming events. The night before the barn fire, she'd warned Ross that something was about to happen. Unfortunately, she had not *seen* enough details to predict exactly what would actually occur. If the housekeeper was now dreaming about Linc's mother, it had to mean something.

"I've known for a long time that Linc's father, Randolf, had passed away. I don't know any of the circumstances around his mother. Is she still living?"

Once again, Marina lifted her brown eyes toward the heavens. "Only God knows that, Nevada."

Nevada looked at her thoughtfully. "You mean, Linc doesn't hear from her? He doesn't know about his own mother?"

Shaking her head, Marina muttered in a disgusted voice, "She left here a long time ago, after Randolf died. Had a new husband on her arm. And she wanted Linc to go with them."

Nevada's gaze drifted thoughtfully to the next ridge of mountain where the tiled top of the big ranch house could be seen above the treetops.

"He didn't go?" she asked.

With another shake of her head, Marina answered, "No. His home, his family had always been here. She couldn't have dragged that boy away from his horses and his cousins to go live somewhere on the east coast. She should have known better. And I expect she did. But she wanted to get away from here—no matter about her son," Marina added with a disapproving sniff. "She was a hard woman to understand. Guess that's 'cause she never did talk much. Linc got that from her. But that's about all he got from that woman."

Nevada was beginning to get the picture and it was one she didn't like. "Well, I wouldn't worry about your dreams, Marina. Sounds like Darla Ketchum is totally out of the picture and has been for some time. I seriously doubt Linc's mood is connected to her in any way."

Marina grimaced. "Darla Ketchum may be out of the picture now, but she could always come back."

Nevada resisted the urge to look over her shoulder to make sure Linc was still in his chair on the porch. "Were you serious when you said no one knew whether she was alive?"

"That's the truth. As far as I know, no one has heard from her in many years." Marina shook her head back and forth. "Linc's a private man, though. If he received any kind of communication from his mother, the rest of us on the ranch might not ever hear about it."

That wasn't surprising news to Nevada. She figured getting anything personal out of him would be worse than trying to give a toddler a dose of medicine.

"Are you two going to yap out there all evening?" Linc suddenly called from the porch. "Or do we get to eat some time before midnight?"

"See," Marina said through tight lips as she looked beyond Nevada's shoulder to the porch. "Listen to him. That's not the Linc I've always known and loved."

Seeing the woman was truly concerned, Nevada patted her shoulder. "Quit worrying, Marina. He'll come out of this, I promise."

The other woman reached into the truck cab to retrieve the box of food. "I hope you're right, *chica.* If anyone can get him back to normal it ought to be you."

Nevada didn't know what normal was for Linc Ketchum, but for everyone's sake she was going to try to find it.

After handing the box to Nevada, Marina climbed into the truck and started the engine.

"You don't want to go say hello to him?" Nevada asked her as the housekeeper ground the gearshift into Reverse.

"No. Tell him I don't like him no more."

"Marina!" Nevada scolded. "You ought—"

"I'm only kidding. But it won't hurt him to think I'm a little put out with him.

Maybe it'll get his mind off himself." She grinned then and gunned the truck down the hill.

Nevada waved the housekeeper off and then headed to the house. As she stepped up on the porch, Linc was eyeing her thoughtfully.

"I didn't realize you were chummy with Marina. You know her?"

"Of course. I've treated her in the clinic. And I've also visited the ranch several times. Her husband was a distant cousin to my father. Both of them sorry men," she added matter-of-factly, then inclined her head toward the door. "Let's go in and eat. I'm starving."

He followed her into the house and on to the kitchen. She set the boxed meal on the table and began to pull out the plastic containers that Marina had sealed it in.

"I'll get plates," he said, turning toward the row of oak cabinets.

Nevada's mouth opened as she looked over her shoulder to voice a protest, but just as quickly she stopped herself. She'd bandaged his hands and fingers thickly enough to provide a cushion. It wouldn't hurt anything to allow him to carry a couple of plates to the table. And would probably do his mental attitude a wealth of good.

"It looks like she's even sent iced tea," Nevada told him. "Is that all right with you?"

"Anything wet will be fine."

He returned to the table carrying two plates, forks and knives and placed one setting at the end of the table and the other across from it. Apparently, Nevada thought, he'd rather have her sitting across from him than right next to him.

Well, that was all right with her. She didn't need to be any closer to the man than she had to be. Something about him made her edgy and flushed, and it didn't have anything to do with his caustic remarks. But she figured it had a whole lot to do with his hard, handsome face and lean, rugged body. One look at him and anyone could see he was a man's man. His body was hewn from years of manual labor, and she realized his physical build was a heck of a lot sexier than some of her male friends who constantly worked out at the gym.

After Nevada poured the tea into glasses and fetched napkins and salt and pepper from the cabinets, the two of them sat down and began to fill their plates.

"Do you think you can manage all right?" Nevada asked. "I can fill your plate for you if you'd like."

His lips a tight line, Linc shook his head. "I'll clean up whatever I spill."

Nevada sighed. "I wasn't worried about that. I don't want you hurting yourself."

"By lifting a spoon with some vegetables in it?" he asked sarcastically.

Exasperated, she waved a dismissive hand at him. "Go ahead. What do I care if your fingers split open? Victoria will probably fire me, is all."

"Worried about your job, are you?"

Normally, Nevada could hold her temper—especially around trying patients. But something about Linc Ketchum really got under her skin and heated her to the boiling point. In spite of his vulnerable condition, she wanted to whack him.

Tossing down her fork, she looked at him. "I think I've had just about enough of you for one evening."

"Think you're about ready to pack up and head back into town?"

As Nevada looked at him she suddenly realized he'd been goading her on purpose, testing her just to see if she was weak-willed enough to bend and run. Well, he was certainly in for a shock if he expected her to quit anything. She wasn't a quitter.

"No. I'd just like to eat my meal without getting indigestion. I'll take my plate to the porch and eat. If you don't mind. Or even if you do."

She started to rise to her feet and was shocked when he reached over and placed his bandaged hand on her arm.

"Sit down."

"I'm not sure I want to."

"Sit down anyway."

Nevada plopped her plate back onto the

table, then reached across and plucked the brown cowboy hat from his head.

"Hey! What do you think you're doing?" he practically yelled at her.

She placed the hat on the bench beside her and tried not to stare at the hair she'd exposed. The chocolate-brown strands were thick and curled recklessly around his head in a way-too-sexy way. And suddenly she was wondering how many women had ever run their fingers through those glossy curls. How many had touched his face and kissed his lips? The questions were not something that crossed her mind about other men and the fact that Linc Ketchum had piqued her curiosity was enough to fill her with embarrassed heat.

Looking down at her plate, she said, "We're eating a meal together. The least you can do is respect me enough to take off your hat."

Linc lifted his hand halfway to his rumpled hair before he realized he couldn't do much finger-combing. Dropping his hand back to the table he glanced across the table to her. He felt like a damn idiot for being so nasty with her. But something seemed to be pushing him to say things to her that he'd never say to anyone, much less a beautiful woman like Nevada. He wasn't sure what had come over him, but the moment she'd driven up and stepped from her car, he'd felt like a ruffled rooster.

"Nevada?"

This was the first time he'd said her name and the way she looked up at him told Linc the sound of it surprised her.

"Yes," she replied.

Like a boy who'd been naughty but never wanted to admit it, he fought the itch to squirm in his seat. "I...uh...guess I've pretty much acted like an ass since you've arrived."

Her brown eyes flicked warily back and forth across his face and Linc wondered what it would feel like to have her soft little body draped over his and be able to look deep into those liquid brown pools.

"Oh. I don't know that I'd say that.

Maybe a donkey would be more like it," she said in a teasing manner.

The idea that she seemed to take what he dished out and still managed to smile was quite a surprise to Linc. Most women would have already been out the door. Is that what he'd been trying to do? he wondered. Send her away before he had the chance to like her? Really like her?

He sighed. "Earlier you asked me about my personality. I don't know if anyone knows how to describe himself. But I do know that since you arrived you haven't been seeing my normal self. I've behaved badly and I'm sorry about it."

The last thing Nevada had been expecting from him was an apology and for long moments she sat studying his rugged face.

"There's no need for you to apologize, Linc. I understand how it is to be unable to work, to do all the things you like to do."

His expression sober, he worked to maneuver the fork between his bandaged fingers. "Being temporarily incapacitated doesn't give me the right to be rude or forget my manners."

"Sometimes it does," she said softly.

"You're too damn understanding. You know that?"

Smiling, she rose from the bench and eased around the table until she was standing next to his shoulder. "Here," she offered, "let me cut the meat up for you."

He wanted to tell her that he was a big, strong man. He didn't need a flirty little thing like her to feed him. But he couldn't. Not if he wanted to enjoy Marina's smothered steak.

Handing his knife and fork up to her he said, "Go ahead before I have the whole plate in my lap."

She chuckled. "You'll do better soon. The more you try to bend your fingers the more flexible they'll become. And tomorrow evening when we redo the bandages it might be possible that I can make the gauze just a bit thinner. That should help, too."

She leaned across him to reach his plate and Linc was suddenly swamped with the female scent of her skin and hair and the warmth of her body that was so very, very close she was practically touching him.

"I hope so," he said thickly.

Long seconds passed as she cut the steak into bite-size pieces. Linc tried his best to keep his breathing even and his mind on anything but her. But it didn't work and eventually the whole lower half of his body was standing at rigid attention.

"There you go," she said. "Think you can manage the fork?"

Linc released a long breath as she finished the task and moved away from him. "I can manage," he muttered.

While he'd been in the hospital, he'd been dependent on the nurses to feed him. But Nevada was a hell of a sight different than any of the nurses that had cared for him and there was no way he could endure her feeding him bite after bite until his plate was empty.

"Well, you have to start somewhere," she said as she took her seat across from him. "I guess tonight is as good as any."

Without looking at her, Linc somehow managed to maneuver the fork between his bandaged thumb and forefinger. Once he had it positioned, he discovered it wasn't all that difficult to push it into the piles of food on his plate.

For the next few minutes the two of them concentrated on eating until Nevada finally glanced across the table at him.

"Victoria told me that you normally live in the bunkhouse with the hands that are quartered here on the ranch. But she didn't say why." She looked around the kitchen with its beautiful oak cabinets and up-to-date appliances. "Why don't you live in this house? Or in the big house with Ross and Bella?"

He didn't bother to glance up. "Because I like being around the guys. They're like family, too. Ross and Bella are great. But they're newlyweds. They don't need another person in the house with them."

Nevada studied him thoughtfully. "I'm aware of how big that house is. They'd never know you were around, unless you wanted them to know it."

"I don't belong in that house," he said curtly.

Her brows inched upward, yet Linc didn't see her reaction to his remark. He appeared to be completely obsessed with the food on his plate.

"Why? You're a Ketchum, too."

"Yes. I'm a Ketchum. But I'm not Tucker's son."

"So what? I don't think your cousins want to split hairs over that issue."

He looked up at her, his eyes thoughtful as they roamed her pretty face.

"What would you know about it?"

She shrugged one shoulder as she lifted a piece of steak to her mouth and chewed. After she'd swallowed the bite, she answered, "Maybe I can't speak for the men of the family, but I can speak for Victoria. She considers you the same as her brother. She thinks you're Mr. Wonderful."

A faint grin came and went on his face. "So you told me before. She's misguided, but you're right. None of them have ever shown me any difference because I was Randolf's son. And before your little head starts spinning, I'll tell you that, no, I don't go around with a chip on my shoulder or anything. I live in the bunkhouse because I like it. There isn't any need for me to live in the big house or in this house. Why would one man take up all this space?" he asked as he motioned a hand around his head.

"I see your point," she said, then a curious frown wrinkled her forehead. "Who built this house anyway? And why? It's far too nice to be just a rental."

Releasing a heavy breath, he leaned back in his chair and looked at her. "You are a nosey little thing, aren't you?"

Nevada smiled at him. "Yes. I guess you could say that. I like learning about the people I care for. It makes it nicer. And—" she broke off as she glanced away from him, then began again. "In nursing school we're taught not to get close to or attached to our patients. But in reality that's a bunch of hogwash. A real nurse feels for the person she's caring for. If she didn't—well, she wouldn't be human."

The idea of Nevada Ortiz getting close or attached to Linc made warning bells clang loudly in his head. It was okay for Victoria to love him as a brother and consider him Mr. Wonderful. She was his cousin. But a woman like Nevada was a different matter altogether. She was beautiful and sexy and the kind of female that could easily make a man forget he was supposed to be a loner.

Feeling it was far safer to talk about the house than nurse/patient relationships, he said, "My father built this house about twenty-five years ago."

Her brown eyes widened with total fascination. "Really? That long ago?"

Linc nodded. "You see my Uncle Tucker and he were partners and started building this ranch together in the late fifties and early sixties. The two of them built the big house first. And that's one of the reasons it has so many wings. Both families lived there together. But then my dad developed a bad heart problem and was no longer able to do the physical labor of a rancher. He sold his half of the ranch to Tucker and built this house for himself and my mom."

"I see. Is that what eventually took your father? Heart disease?"

For a second time, Linc nodded and Nevada could see a regretful shadow cross his face.

"Yeah. I was just a teenager. It hit me pretty hard. We were buddies, my dad and I. He was a gifted horseman and taught me everything he knew about the animals."

A smile touched Nevada's lips. "It must have been very nice to have had a father like that."

"Yeah. But I lost him way too early." He awkwardly stabbed his fork into a piece of steak. "My dad was a quiet, gentle man. He never raised his voice or hurt anyone. Now my Uncle Tucker was just the opposite. My cousins would be the first to tell you he was a hellish rounder. Two different men, but they both died of bad hearts. Guess I should make sure I eat right," he said with a bit of dark humor.

Nevada wasn't going to start preaching to him about how he could be genetically prone to heart disease. Now wasn't the time to be a nurse. Tonight she was talking to Linc as a woman and a friend.

She carefully sipped her tea, then dared to ask, "You don't ever communicate with your mother?"

He glanced up at her through narrowed eyes. "Who told you that?"

Her tanned cheeks turned a hot pink. "Marina," she confessed.

Linc snorted. "Marina is just like a tape recorder. She doesn't forget anything and if you push the right buttons, she'll repeat it all."

Nevada put her fork down. "I'm sorry if I shouldn't have brought up the subject of your mother."

"Don't worry about it," he muttered as he turned his attention to the food left on his plate. "There's nothing to tell about her anyway. We don't talk."

"Oh. I'm sorry."

"No need to be sorry." He lifted his eyes

to hers. "There wouldn't be much point in trying to communicate with a woman who's only capable of thinking about herself."

Questions pummeled her from every direction. But she managed to stifle them all, except one. "Is that what you think about all women?"

His lips twisted to a mocking slant. "I have more important things to think about than women."

After that sardonic remark, Nevada didn't bother to attempt to make more conversation. She finished her meal then excused herself from the table to gather makings for coffee.

She was waiting for it to drip when she turned around to see that Linc had left the table and slipped out of the kitchen. Which was just as well, Nevada thought. He'd made it clear that he didn't put much stock in a woman's company.

The idea that any man could be so callous and cynical was enough to snap Nevada's back teeth together in an angry grind. But then she quickly scolded herself for allowing his attitude to rile her. She wasn't here to socialize with the man. Or even to like him as a person. Her job was simply to care for his burns and his physical needs. And from now on that was all she intended to do.

Chapter Five

Once the coffee was ready to serve, Nevada poured two cups and carried them out of the kitchen. The living room was empty, so she stepped out on the porch to see if Linc had returned to his willow chair.

Sure enough, she found him there. His boots were crossed at the ankles, his gaze on the moon rising above the eastern mesas.

"I wasn't sure whether you liked coffee or not. But I brought you a cup anyway," she told him. "It's black."

He looked around to where she stood by the screen door and Nevada could see a flicker of surprise cross his face.

"You needn't have bothered," he told her. "I would have gotten it later."

"No bother."

She handed him the cup and made sure he could manage holding it before she turned back toward the door.

"Where are you going?"

The question caught her totally off guard and she paused long enough to glance over her shoulder at him. "Inside. I—have some reading to do."

"Oh."

"If you need anything I'll be in my room," she told him, then went into the house before he could say more.

She had just gotten comfortable with her book when the telephone near the head of her bed rang. Nevada tossed the book to one side and rolled across the mattress to lift the receiver.

"Hello."

"Nevada, it's Victoria. I just wanted to check and see how things have been going. Is Linc there with you?"

Nevada sat up on the side of the bed. "He's outside on the porch. He can't hear what I say."

"Good. Then tell me how things went. Has he been giving you a difficult time?"

Nevada breathed in deeply then slowly released it. Linc Ketchum was like no man she'd ever encountered before. She'd never had a man make her so angry one moment, then filled with empathy the next.

"When you said you wanted a favor from me, you meant a *big* favor," she said wryly.

"Oh dear. He's been that bad?" Victoria asked with concern.

"No. Not exactly. But he is—well, he isn't ordinary, I'll say that much."

Victoria sighed. "You have to understand, Nevada, that Linc isn't your ordinary man. He's not like the other single ranch hands on the T Bar K. Outside of his horses, he doesn't have much of a life. And now the burns have taken that away. Just be as gentle as you can be without losing your mind. I promise, you'll get a big bonus out of this."

Nevada frowned. She hadn't taken this job for money. In fact, she really didn't want extra pay for it. She already owed

Victoria so much for giving her such a special job at the clinic.

"I'm not concerned about any of that," she told the doctor.

"Nonsense. You've always dreamed about taking a vacation to Hawaii. When all of this is over with I'm going to make sure you're going."

Under any other circumstances, Nevada would have been shouting for joy at the idea of heading to the tropical island. But something just didn't feel right about using Linc's misfortune for her gain. "We'll talk about that later," Nevada told her.

"Okay. Is there anything you need? Something you might have forgotten to take with you? A book on patience?" Victoria teased.

Nevada had to laugh. "Oh, he hasn't been all that bad," she tried to assure the other woman. "Just a little bad. And I'm dealing with it."

"That's good. I know you will, Nevada. And I still believe you'll be the best medicine for Linc."

Nevada chuckled with disbelief. "Apparently you don't know your cousin too well. He doesn't like women."

Aghast, Victoria asked, "He told you that?"

"Not in so many words. But it meant the same."

Victoria didn't reply for several long seconds, then she said, "Linc doesn't trust too many women."

Nevada grimaced. "That's obvious. He—uh—he told me a little about his mother. Well, it was very little. But he said she'd only thought about herself and that the two of them didn't communicate. Is that true, Victoria?"

This time an even longer pause passed before Victoria responded. "Linc talked to you about his mother?"

"Yes. Why?"

"Well, frankly, I'm shocked. He doesn't speak about her to anyone. Even in a remote way."

Surprise parted Nevada's lips. "Oh. I didn't realize."

"What did you do to the man anyway?"

"Victoria, what kind of question is that? I didn't do *anything* to the man!"

Victoria laughed softly in her ear. "I meant what did you do to get him talking."

"Irritated him, I think."

"Well, it sounds like you're doing the right thing. Just keep it up. Now, how about you? Are you comfortable enough? Did you find everything in the house you needed?"

"Yes. My room is lovely. Everything is fine." Except that each time I look at your cousin my pulse does silly flip-flops, Nevada silently added.

"Good," Victoria told her. "Then maybe the next couple of weeks or so won't seem like being in prison to you."

Nevada assured the other woman that she didn't feel locked away and then the conversation turned to work at the clinic and for the next few minutes they spoke of other patients and problems.

Eventually, baby Sam began to cry in the background and Victoria ended the conversation to see about her son.

Nevada hung up the telephone and reached for her book while wondering what it would feel like to go home every night to a husband and children.

When she looked at Victoria's life, it all seemed so wonderful. Even though her husband, Jess, was a lawman and often had to work odd hours, he made sure that he and Victoria spent special time together and Victoria did the same for him. Their children were the center of their lives and when they were all together Nevada could see a glow of love encircling the family.

But as far as Nevada was concerned, the Hastings weren't the norm. Most of her young married friends often complained about philandering, selfishness, fights and everything else that happened when a male and female butted heads.

Nevada didn't want that for herself. She'd already seen too much of it as a child. And she realized the chance of finding a special love like Victoria and Jess had was minuscule. She wasn't willing to gamble her heart with those sorts of odds. No matter how lonely she became.

Later, after Nevada had finally managed to read several chapters of her paperback, she got up from the bed and changed into a pair of black pajamas and a white robe trimmed in black.

She was pulling a hairbrush through her long hair when she heard a soft tapping on her bedroom door and went to open it.

Linc was standing on the other side of the threshold. His expression was just a bit disgusted and a little apologetic.

"Were you asleep?" he asked.

Nevada lifted the hairbrush for him to see. "Brushing my hair. But I was thinking about going to bed. Do you need something?"

He grimaced as though her question was inane. "Hell, yes!" he burst out, then with a dismal shake of his head he apologized. "Sorry, Nevada. I'm just feeling too damn helpless, that's all. I need for you to help me get undressed. I managed to slip off my boots. But the shirt and the jeans are another matter. I tried to work the buttons loose, but the bandages are still too thick to catch hold of something so small."

"Oh, Linc," she said contritely, "I'm so sorry! I'd forgotten all about your clothing. And you must be getting tired."

He wasn't exactly tired, Linc thought. In fact, he couldn't remember a time he'd felt so worked up and restless. He felt as if he could jump at least ten barbed-wire fences and never get a scratch. Which was a damn stupid feeling for a man his age.

"Yeah. It's been a long day," he replied as casually as he could.

"Just let me put away my brush, and if you want to go across to your room, I'll be right there."

He nodded, and she whirled back into her room. Linc released a shaky breath as he turned and walked into his own bedroom.

Damn it, he thought, as he switched on a lamp next to the head of the bed. He shouldn't be feeling so nervous about any of this. He'd had women undress him before. And most any man would be envious of his position—a young, beautiful woman taking off his clothes. But he wasn't like most men. And Nevada surely wasn't like most nurses.

When Nevada knocked lightly on the door, he was trying to decide whether it would be best to sit down on the bed or stand. He very nearly jumped at the sound and quickly muttered a curse at himself. She wasn't going to eat him. And he wasn't going to bite her. The two of them weren't like the mares and stallions he bred for the ranch's remuda.

"Come in," he called gruffly.

The room was L-shaped and she stuck her head around the corner and shot him a brief smile. "Ready?" she asked.

"Well, I don't want to sleep in my clothes," he assured her.

Ignoring the sarcastic tone of his remark, Nevada moved into the bedroom and went to stand in front of him. The light by the bed was fashioned from a stack of horse-shoes and shaded with a thin sheet of rawhide. The illumination slanting across the two of them was muted but enough for Nevada to see where the buttons on his shirt started and ended.

She reached for the first one and quickly slipped it through the slot. The fabric of his shirt was starched and crisp, a stark contrast to his warm smooth skin. She tried her best to keep her fingers from touching his chest. Not only for his sake, but her own, too. Yet it was virtually impossible to maneuver the buttons without having her fingers touch his skin. Each time she did, her hands received a sizzling jolt and she wondered if he was feeling any of the same sort of reactions she was experiencing.

One, two, three, four. Finally, she reached the eighth button and the two pieces of fabric fell apart. Barely glancing at the skin above his belt, she said, "Now hold your arms out slightly so that I can pull the sleeves down over your bandages. I don't want to disturb the gauze."

He did as she instructed and Nevada carefully pushed the shirt off his shoulders until it draped against his back. By the time she'd moved to the sleeves, she was struggling to keep her breathing at an even keel. The physical reaction she was having to Linc totally shocked her and though she'd assured him that undressing him wouldn't turn her face red, she felt heat seeping into every inch of her body, including her cheeks.

Linc stood stock-still and barely breathing as her hands slowly and carefully worked the sleeves down one arm and then the other. Each time her fingers brushed against his skin, the muscles in his throat clenched to rigid bands. He tried to put his thoughts on other things, but he couldn't think about the weather, his horses or the men down at the bunkhouse when every particle inside him wanted to reach out and touch this woman standing before him.

"Can't you hurry this up," he said with a faint growl. "The roosters are going to be crowing before I ever get to bed."

She looked up at him, her expression turning sardonic. "You'll get there soon enough. Besides, I doubt there's a rooster within miles of here."

He grunted a laugh. "Don't leave your window up tonight. Marina has two roosters and both of them like to crow."

"Don't all men," she muttered under her breath.

"What?"

She drew in a long breath and blew it out. "Nothing. I'll keep the windows shut. By the way, what time do you get up?"

He looked down at her. "Normally I get up at four-thirty. But that's when I'm working. Why does it matter?"

"Do you want to walk around the house in your underwear? Or would you like me to help you get into your jeans first?" she asked dryly.

Oh Lord, he thought desperately. This whole dressing and undressing thing was going to have to go on for several days. Probably until the bandages on his fingers came off completely. And after looking at their fragile appearance tonight, he doubted that would be any time soon.

He didn't answer immediately and she spoke up before he could decide exactly what he wanted to tell her.

"Maybe I should send for some sweat pants or pajamas. You could pull them on yourself and not have to endure me touching you." The shirt finally slipped down his arm and she tossed the garment onto the bed.

Linc's brows shot upward at her testy remark. "Who said I didn't want you touching me?"

"I can tell. It's killing you."

It was killing him all right, but not in the way she was thinking, Linc thought dismally. He had not expected any of this to feel so intimate and personal. He certainly hadn't expected this deep desire to reach out and touch her hair, her skin, her face.

"You're a nurse. This is your job," he pointed out more for himself than her.

"That's right. I've done this very thing many times before," she said matter-of-factly as she reached for the button on the waistband of his jeans. "It's all old hat."

He sucked in such a sharp breath it was as if someone had taken a knife to his throat. "I'll bet."

Nevada's lips twisted and she glanced up at him with hard brown eyes. "That's the second time you've implied that I'm promiscuous. What gave you that idea?"

"You. You said you had boyfriends. Or did I misunderstand you?"

With a shake of her head, she focused her gaze on the fly of his jeans. "No. You didn't misunderstand. And aren't you glad I've got experience. Otherwise, I might just get you all tangled up in this zipper," she added cattily.

Linc started to growl a warning at her, but the loud sound of the zipper peeling open caused his mouth to snap shut. Now wasn't the time to press his luck, he thought. And if she didn't step away from him soon, and leave the room, he was going to do something crazy. Like grab her and kiss her until she couldn't say one more sassy word to him.

She yanked the jeans down over his

hips then put her palm in the middle of his chest. "Sit down on the bed and I'll pull them off," she ordered.

He looked down at her soft brown hand pressing against his flesh, then lifted his gaze to hers. Something about the way she was touching him, looking at him, stirred him in ways he'd never experienced before and the feelings shocked and scared him. She was seducing him without even trying and he wanted to yell at her to get out and leave him alone. He didn't want a woman turning his insides out. Especially not a woman who enjoyed playing the field.

He sat down and Nevada grabbed onto the hem of his jeans and tugged the heavy denim down over his feet. Once they were free of his body, she tossed them onto his shirt and stepped back, noticing thankfully that he was wearing a pair of white boxers loose enough to hide the shape of his manhood.

Clearing her throat, she asked as professionally as she could, "Is there anything else you need? Can you turn the covers back without my help?"

"Yeah," he muttered, "I can manage."

She looked across the room to where the curtains fluttered in the night breeze. "Do you normally sleep with the windows open?"

He glanced over his shoulder to follow her gaze. "Yes. When the nights are cool, we usually keep the bunkhouse open. But that doesn't mean that you have to turn off the air conditioner," he assured her. "I'm sure you're accustomed to artificial heating and cooling. I wouldn't want you to be uncomfortable just for my sake."

If his words had been sincere she would have been drawn to his thoughtfulness. But the sarcasm in his voice told her that he apparently had the idea that she was a spoiled princess who fooled around. The idea was laughable, yet at the moment she couldn't find it in her to be amused.

"I'm not concerned about myself," she said coolly. "If you're not accustomed to sleeping in a draft, you'll wind up with a cold. And that's the last thing your body needs when its trying to repair itself."

Even in the muted light, she could see his gaze flicking up and down her body. The sight caused her to unconsciously tighten the lapels of her robe together.

"I'll be fine," he said curtly.

"Good. I'll say good-night, then."

Turning, she started to leave the room. But before she rounded the corner that would hide her from his view, he called her name.

Pausing, she stifled a sigh and wondered how she'd ever gotten into such an awkward ordeal.

Nevada glanced over her shoulder at him just in time to see him swallow and she was suddenly struck with the fact that he was nervous, that her touch had left him just as unsettled as she was feeling. The idea made her look at him in a totally different way and she felt her heart softening in spite of all the tacky comments he'd said to her.

"Thanks," he said quietly. "I appreciate your help."

Turning slightly back to him, she said, "You sure have a funny way of expressing it."

He grimaced. "Don't expect me to be good at communicating, Nevada. I do most of my talking to horses and they're much smarter than humans. Just a few words to them gets the point across."

Curious now, she walked back to him. "Is that really true? Do horses understand what you're saying?"

A soft glow lit his dark-green eyes. "Hell yes, they understand. In fact, most of the time you don't have to say a word. They just know what you want even before you do."

She smiled wanly. "That sounds very nice. To be understood. But then I guess most animals have that inner instinct. I don't know anything about horses. I've only ridden twice in my life."

"That's a shame."

In the back of her mind, Nevada knew she shouldn't be standing here in Linc's bedroom, talking to him about anything other than his physical condition or needs. But she understood that he needed to talk, he needed to realize that sharing his thoughts with another person could actually be a nice experience.

"While I was growing up several of my friends had horses, but my family couldn't afford to have a horse. I felt left out when they got together and went on rides."

"Your family was poor?"

She nodded. "Not dirt-poor. But we didn't have much for any sort of extras."

His gaze was beginning to wander over her face and hair and she could feel her stomach doing silly little jumps and twirls. He was an extremely handsome man. Not in a suave or smooth way, but in a very, very masculine way and she could hardly keep her eyes off his broad, thick shoulders or wide expanse of chest sprinkled with curly brown hair.

"How did you manage to go to nursing school?" he asked.

"I worked my way through with different part-time jobs. I worked in a dry cleaners, a café, a pharmacy, an insurance office. The last one paid the best, but I hated it. The day was filled with people demanding money and threatening lawsuits. It wasn't for me. But at least it kept my bills and tuition paid. And I received a couple of scholarships that helped get me through."

"What about your parents? They didn't help with your education?"

Nevada shook her head. "Mom does well to take care of herself. And Dad left a long time ago. He calls and comes around once in a while, but that's about it." Her gaze dropped to her bare toes. "He always figured I'd take care of myself. And I always have."

Linc tried to tell himself that her accomplishments weren't that big a deal. It wasn't uncommon for women to succeed on their own. Yet that was usually after they were grown and standing on secure ground. He figured Nevada had scrapped and scraped from the time she was big enough to work at odd jobs. He admired her greatly for that, even if he didn't like her list of boyfriends.

"Uh—I know I can't do anything with the horses now. But later on you might like to take a ride." He didn't add, *with me*. He told himself he wasn't necessarily making the offer as a way to spend time with her. He wanted to pay her back in some way and a horseback ride was as common as breathing to him.

A slow grin lifted the corners of her lips and Linc realized he'd like to kiss those corners until her lips parted and her eyelids drifted shut.

"You must already be planning how to pay me back," she said teasingly. "I guess you've already got your worst bronc in mind to put me on."

That brought a smile to his face. "There's not a horse in my remuda that's a bronc. They're not bred to buck. They're bred to work cattle."

He leaned over to the nightstand and opened a door at the bottom. Several books were stacked inside and his bandaged hand shuffled awkwardly through them until he reached the one he was searching for.

"Here," he said, offering the book out to her. "You might like to look through this. If you're not interested, that's all right, too."

Nevada stepped forward and took the book from him. *"The American Quarter Horse,"* she read aloud, then glanced at him. "Is that what you raise here on the ranch?"

He nodded.

Smiling, she clutched the book to her breasts. "Thank you, Linc. I'll take this to bed with me."

As Linc watched her leave his bedroom he couldn't help but wonder what it would be like if she took him to bed. But that wasn't something he could allow his mind to dwell on. Because going to bed with Nevada Ortiz was something that would never, ever happen.

Chapter Six

The next morning when Nevada climbed out of bed, the first thing that caught her attention was the smell of coffee. Which could only mean that Linc was already up and in the kitchen. How he'd managed to make coffee with his bandaged hands, she didn't know, but she was certainly going to find out.

After a quick trip to the bathroom, she tied on her robe and stuck her feet into a pair of satin mules. Once she left the bedroom, she headed straight to the kitchen expecting to find Linc there, but the room was empty.

She poured herself a cup of coffee, which still smelled quite fresh, stirred in a hefty amount of cream, then walked over to the back door to glance onto the patio.

The sight of Linc sitting there in a green motel chair took her by complete surprise. A moment ago, when she'd discovered he wasn't in the kitchen, she'd assumed he'd be on the front porch. He seemed to feel more comfortable outdoors and probably enjoyed drinking his morning coffee in the fresh air. She hadn't expected to find him at the back of the house.

Opening the door, she stepped down onto the patio and carried her coffee over to where he sat with his long legs out in front of him. He hadn't bothered to put on his hat and the faint yellow glow of the rising sun made the brown strands glisten with streaks of gold. The shirt he was wearing wasn't buttoned. Neither were his jeans, but she could see he'd somehow managed to zip them up enough to keep them on his hips.

"Good morning," she greeted him while telling herself not to notice how damn sexy he looked. Those broad thick shoulders and square jaw didn't make up for his moodiness, she told herself. Besides, he'd been a bachelor for years and from all that she could tell, he didn't much like women. It would be foolish of her to fantasize about the man.

"Good morning," he replied.

"Sorry I wasn't up to help you dress," she told him. "Why didn't you wake me?"

Linc glanced over as she took a seat in a nearby lawn chair. Her white satin robe clung to every curve of her body and her black hair draped her shoulders like wild, tangled vines. The makeup she'd been wearing yesterday had been washed away and now he could see the true smoothness of her rosy-tan cheeks and the long silkiness of her lashes. Her lips reminded him of dark-pink roses, the kind his aunt Amelia used to grow in a sheltered corner of the big house garden.

Nevada Ortiz was a naturally beautiful woman, he thought. Just like the rising of the sun in the azure New Mexican sky.

"It wasn't necessary to wake you," he said after a moment.

"You've been using your hands too much," she scolded. "When I unwrap them this evening, I'd better not find that you've disturbed the skin, or you and I will both be in big-time trouble. I really don't relish being chewed out by two doctors."

"Two doctors?"

"Dr. Olstead and Dr. Hastings," she explained.

"Don't worry," he said with a faint frown. "I haven't put a lot of pressure on my fingers. They feel fine. In fact, I think they're a little more flexible this morning."

Studying him over the rim of her coffee cup, she was surprised to see he appeared relaxed this morning. The grim, tight expression he'd worn most of yesterday was gone and his green eyes were much softer. She was happy to see the change in him, yet at the same time she realized that like this, he was much more dangerous to her well-being.

"Good. I'm glad. You're going to be

surprised how quickly you heal. I know it probably seems like you've been bundled up in bandages for a long time now. But later, when you look back on all of this, you'll realize it wasn't all that long. And it certainly beats being turned into a charred piece of toast." She sipped her coffee, then glanced at him from the corner of her eye, "Do you think the fire was an accident?"

He frowned as he continued to watch the glow of morning sunlight breaking over the red mesas. "I really don't know. The barn was built back in the sixties and had been updated through the years. In fact, the electrical wiring was replaced only last year. I can't imagine what might have set off the flames. But I can't imagine anyone deliberately setting the building on fire. Not with helpless mares locked inside their stalls." His jaw turned to granite. "But if it was arson, I'd want to kill the bastard."

The tone of his voice was just menacing enough to have Nevada studying him even closer. Even though he was man who kept to himself, she figured he wouldn't be bashful about going after any one who'd crossed him.

"Well," she said, "I'm sure it was an accident." She was silent a moment as she remembered the other well-publicized goings on at the T Bar K... "But so many things have happened on the T Bar K this past year it makes a person wonder if something else might be going on."

"Yeah. I thought the same, too."

Nevada thoughtfully turned her attention to her coffee and for the next few minutes the two of them sat in silence as the magpies sang from a nearby pine tree.

The solitude of being in the mountains and alone with Linc was something altogether different for Nevada. Aztec wasn't a busy metropolis by any means, but it was a darn sight more active than this place. At this time of the morning, she was usually already up and dressed and hurrying to work with one hand on the steering wheel while she tried to gulp down a cup of coffee with the other. Patients of all ages from cranky adults to crying babies would be crammed into the waiting room of the clinic and she would have to deal with each one kindly and methodically before Dr. Hastings made her entrance into the examining room.

Every day was a busy day for Nevada. And not too many of her nights were spent alone in front of the television. More often than not, she went out with friends to a movie or dinner, or a nearby concert. In her opinion, life was too fun and too short to spend it alone.

Yet there was something cozy and extremely intimate about sitting here in the morning sun and wearing only a robe and pajamas while a sinfully sexy man lounged mere inches away. And the fact that his jeans and shirt weren't buttoned only added to the pleasant picture around her.

"I'm getting hungry," he said suddenly. "Do you know how to cook breakfast?"

So much for leisurely sipping her coffee, Nevada thought wryly. But then she wasn't here to sit around admiring her patient. This was a job, not a romantic getaway.

"Sure I do. My mother could hardly boil water, but my grandmother is a wonderful cook and she made me work in the kitchen from the time I was a small girl. She said a woman would never be out of a job if she knew how to cook." Nevada tossed him a wry grin. "Thankfully, I'm past being the grill cook at the Wagon Wheel."

Surprise marked his face. "You worked at the Wagon Wheel as a cook?"

Nodding, she carefully rose from the chair while balancing her coffee cup. "For about a year. Remember? I told you I worked in a café."

"Yeah. But I didn't know your job was cook and I didn't know it was at the Wagon Wheel. They always have good food."

She chuckled. "Thanks for the vote of confidence. In a few minutes you can judge for yourself if I've lost my touch."

Nevada left him on the patio and went to her bedroom to dress. She wasn't about to cook breakfast in her night clothes. That would be behaving too much like a wife. And she certainly didn't want Linc to get the notion that she had that kind of idea about him or any man. Lord, what an embarrassing situation that would be.

Pulling on a pair of blue jeans and a pale-yellow T-shirt that buttoned down the front, she fastened her long hair at the nape of her neck with a brown tortoiseshell barrette. After a quick dab of face powder and lipstick, she hurried out to the kitchen and began to assemble the fixings for breakfast.

She was frying bacon and link sausage when she heard the back door open and close, then Linc's footsteps grow closer and closer before they stopped somewhere behind her.

His nearness caused the nerve endings on Nevada's skin to stand like metal shavings on a magnet and she drew in a deep, bracing breath before she turned to look at him.

"I have things going," she said as she tried to keep her eyes off the strip of bare chest and hard abdomen exposed by the loose tails of his shirt. "How do hot cakes sound? Or would you rather have fried eggs or an omelette?"

This was not the way he'd expected his nurse to be treating him—as though he was royalty and could pick anything from the kitchen that his heart desired. Was she trying to impress him for some reason? he wondered. There wasn't any need for her to lift a hand to prepare meals. Marina would be more than glad to send every meal to them. Especially since she had plenty of leftovers, some of which usually made their way to the bunkhouse. Old Cook wasn't too happy when Marina's treats appeared in his kitchen. He was protective of his position and didn't like it threatened by a woman trying to outshine him. But Nevada was a nurse, she didn't need to stand over a cookstove. Especially for him. And Linc didn't know whether to be pleased by her attitude or wary of her motives.

"Hot cakes sounds good. But—uh— I'd appreciate it if you could button these things up for me."

He gestured down to his shirt. Nevada put down the fork in her hand and stepped toward him. Before she even reached for the two pieces of fabric hanging against his chest, her heart began to beat fast and faint, her breathing slowed to light little sips of air sucked between her parted lips.

"I'm sorry. I should have offered to do this for you sooner," she said in a thick voice.

Linc felt every part of his body going rigid with anticipation as she moved close and took hold of his shirt. This morning she smelled like honeysuckle and morning dew and he wondered if her dark-pink lips would taste just as sweet and moist.

Damn it, he wasn't a man who went around fantasizing about kissing a woman or imagining the shape of her body beneath her clothing, but he seemed to be doing both with Nevada. And he didn't know how he was going to keep his sanity spending this first day with her, much less two weeks.

"That's all right. Maybe I can do it myself pretty soon." Like tomorrow, Linc thought desperately, then sucked in a fiery breath as her small fingers inadvertently brushed against his belly.

Hearing the sharp intake, Nevada dropped her hands and jumped back. "What's wrong? Did I hurt you?" she asked with great concern.

Linc groaned silently. "No. I just had a—sharp pain in one of my hands. It was nothing," he lied. He wasn't about to admit that the touch of her fingers had filled him with more heat than he'd encountered in the burning horse barn.

"Oh. Maybe I should unwrap it and have a look," she suggested as she reached once again for his shirt.

"No, dammit," he said sharply. "It was just a little pain. Nothing to get all shook up about." Only he *was* shook up, Linc thought. He'd been shook up ever since she'd arrived yesterday and the whole idea made him angry at himself and at Victoria for ever sending the woman up here. For two cents he'd call his cousin and tell her to find someone else, that he was going to send Nevada packing. But what would be his excuse? he wondered. That he found her too attractive? That for the first time in his life he'd met a woman he couldn't push out of his mind?

"All right. But please tell me if you have any more of them," she said. "Now if you'll—suck in a bit, I'll button your jeans."

While she worked to fasten the waistband of his jeans, Linc pulled his eyes away from the shiny crown of her head and looked toward the window. This time she couldn't prevent her fingers from touching him and it was all he could do to remain motionless as she searched for the tongue of the zipper nestled just above his crotch.

His heart began to pound like a hammer, forcing hot blood to parts of his body that he wished would remain cold. "If you knew how much I hated this, you'd hurry it up," he finally barked at her. "And I sure as hell don't want burned bacon for breakfast."

Her lips a tight line, she yanked up the

zipper and whirled back to the cookstove. "You think I enjoy dressing you?" she muttered as she whipped the browning bacon on to its other side.

"I don't know. Do you?"

Her mouth fell open as she jerked her head around at him. "Keep asking me questions like that and you can cook your own breakfast the best way you can," she said tightly.

For long, tense moments he stared at her. What the hell was he doing, he wondered. He'd been trying his best to get along with the woman. He didn't really want to insult her. And he sure as heck hadn't meant to ask her such a provocative question. But something strange seemed to happen to him whenever she touched him. His normal personality flew out the window and left behind a rutting buck without any manners.

Raking a bandaged hand over his rumpled hair, he said regretfully, "Aw hell, Nevada. Go ahead and say it. I'm a terrible patient."

Ducking her head, she turned back to the

frying meat and lifted the browned strips onto a plate lined with paper towel. "Forget it. I understand."

Not liking the idea that he'd hurt her feelings, he moved forward and placed his hands on her shoulders. The bandages on his hands prevented him from feeling the heat of her body, the softness of her skin, but he could imagine the sensation and it was enough to cause his stomach to clench with desire.

"Do you?" he asked softly.

Slowly she turned and lifted her face to his. There was a challenging tilt to her chin, but there were also shadows in her dark eyes, expressions that he couldn't understand but desperately wanted to.

"I think so. You don't like me near you. You don't like me touching you."

Linc tried not to flinch. He had not expected anything so blunt to come out of her mouth. And he'd especially not expected her to read him so closely.

"Look, Nevada, it isn't that I don't like you—"

"Liking me has nothing to do with it," she interrupted. "You don't like how I make you feel. And you're afraid that I'm feeling the same way toward you."

Linc swallowed as his throat tightened and his heart continued to chug like a laboring freight train. "Since you seem to know so much about me, just how do I feel?"

As Nevada's gaze roamed his sober face, she realized she shouldn't have gotten into this conversation. It was going to lead them to things that neither of them needed to hear or feel. But there was no way she could avoid his question now without looking like more of a fool than she already did.

"I think you find me attractive," she said frankly.

Slowly, his dark brows inched upward and she shivered with surprise as his bandaged hands slid up the sides of her neck and gently cupped her face.

"And how do you find me, Nevada Ortiz?"

The question was spoken so softly she

could barely hear it. But she did hear and she couldn't ignore it any more than she could dismiss the sudden pounding of her heart.

"You're a very masculine, good-looking man, Linc. I'm sure you've had plenty of women tell you that."

She watched his nostrils flare and for a moment she believed she'd angered him all over again, but then his face softened and his bandaged thumbs began to move back and forth across her cheeks. In the back of her mind, Nevada realized she wanted to feel the touch of his skin upon hers instead of the coarse gauze wrapped around his fingers. She wanted to know what it was like to be in his arms and have his hard lips kissing hers.

"Do you feed the egos of all your male patients like this?"

The corners of her mouth lifted ever so slightly. "I've never had any male patients like you."

A faint grimace twisted his lips. "What

does that mean? That you're still trying to flatter me?"

"I never intended to flatter you. I'm only trying to answer your questions."

"Really."

His one word was full of disbelief and while Nevada's mind was screaming at her to step away from him and put a stop to his touch and the senseless conversation between them, she found that her legs refused to obey her commands.

"That's right," she said as she nervously licked her lips. "I've attended to plenty of male patients over the years. But they were all housed in a hospital room or medical clinic. They were all bedridden or incapacitated in some way. They weren't strong and virile like you."

The more she spoke, the more pink color seeped into her cheeks, and as Linc's gaze roamed her face he realized her blush surprised him. She'd already admitted she'd had plenty of boyfriends. Surely it didn't make her feel self-conscious to talk about the intimate things that went on between a man and a woman.

"That's the way you see me?"

Desire was growing thick in her throat, followed by a choking lump of fear. Just having this man touch her face was making little earthquakes go off inside her. What would happen if he actually put some effort into it, she wondered wildly.

"Stop this, Linc. I can't be your nurse if you're, well, personal like this. It won't work."

"No. It won't work," he murmured lazily. "But I tried to tell you that yesterday. You should have gotten into your car and driven away when I told you to."

His gaze zeroed in on her lips and Nevada felt every bone in her body turning to liquid fire. "So what are you going to do about it?" she muttered inanely.

"What do you think I'm going to do about it?" he asked with a growl.

"Find another nurse to take my place?"

"It's too late for that," he murmured. "And too late for this, too."

Nevada could see his head bending toward hers yet she couldn't believe that he was going to kiss her until she actually felt the touch of his lips.

The contact was like the strike of a match in a pitch-dark room. The space around them seemed to light up and tiny flames sizzled upon her lips as Linc's mouth dominated hers with a bold search that left her breathless and shaking uncontrollably.

Halfway through the kiss, his hands left her face and gathered at the back of her waist. She stumbled slightly as he tugged her forward and into the circle of his arms. The front of her body landed against his and she was instantly consumed with heat and the wild urge to slip her arms around his neck, to hold on and never let go.

She felt the room receding and her senses being sucked into a velvety-soft place when the shrill sound of the telephone jolted the two of them apart.

They stared at each other in shocked silence before Linc finally turned away and clumsily snatched the ringing receiver from the wall near the cabinets.

Nevada sucked in a deep breath and turned back to the skillet on the cookstove. Thank God she'd turned the burner off beneath the sausage or it would have burned to a crisp by now.

As she put a flame beneath the skillet, she realized her hands were trembling and she couldn't seem to suck in enough air to satisfy her lungs. What had the man done to her? She'd been kissed before. Or so she'd thought. Apparently, none of her past suitors had known what they were doing or the chemistry between them had been bad. And that was all it had been between her and Linc, she firmly told herself. Chemistry. Pure and simple. He was a raw male animal and his rough edges excited her sexually. That's all there was to it.

"That was Marina," he said as he hung up the telephone. "She wanted to know if she needed to send breakfast to us."

Nevada wondered how he could sound so normal, so unaffected when her whole body was still vibrating from the kiss they'd shared. But then maybe he hadn't felt any of the things she'd felt, Nevada decided. Maybe the kiss had been just an impulse that he now regretted.

"What did you tell her?" she asked while hating the fact that her own voice was strained.

"Not to bother. That you were cooking up something. I just didn't know what it was yet."

For the next few moments as Nevada broke eggs into another skillet, the innuendo of his remark didn't sink in. When it finally registered that Linc hadn't been referring to breakfast, she turned around to shoot a few choice words at him. But the room was empty.

Nevada was relieved. She didn't need to get into another war of words with the man. And she certainly didn't need to kiss him again. But she very much wanted to. And even worse than that, he probably knew she did.

Chapter Seven

Linc's cousin Ross arrived shortly after they'd finished eating breakfast. The two men sat together on the front porch and drank coffee while Nevada cleaned the kitchen and tried to assure herself that everything was going to be all right.

Throughout the meal, Linc had never mentioned the kiss and neither did she. Maybe it was better that way, she told herself. Maybe if they both behaved as though it had never happened, then they could forget it and move on.

She *had* to move on to the job at hand, Nevada thought. Because Linc was not a man who'd be interested in any sort of relationship with her. From all that she could see, he didn't even much like women. She didn't need to ruin her life by pining over a man who didn't give a flip about her.

Out on the porch, Linc listened to Ross as he talked about his trip to the livestock auction at Farmington yesterday. Normally he was always interested to hear how cattle and horses were selling on the market, but today Ross wasn't holding his attention.

Damn it, he'd been a big, stupid fool to kiss Nevada. Hell, he didn't even know why he had. Except that he'd wanted to kiss her and had ever since she'd stepped out of her car and faced him with her hands on her shapely little hips. Now it was going to be hell to keep his distance from her. But it was something he was going to have to do. Being indisposed with burns was a minor problem compared to the pains Nevada could cause him.

"Linc, are you sure you're feeling all right?"

He looked over to see Ross studying him with a narrow eye.

"Sure. I'm fine. Or I would be if I could

take these damn bandages off and get to work," he answered.

Ross's gaze leveled on Linc's bandaged arms and hands. "Yeah. I guess that would be hell going around like that," he said, then grinned mischievously, "but it might not be all bad to have Bella doing everything for me. Like giving me a bath, helping me dress—"

He broke off suddenly and Linc stared purposely out at the mountain range in the far distance.

"Oh. So that's what's bothering you," Ross said with sudden decisiveness. "You don't like having Miss Ortiz getting that personal."

He turned a glare on his cousin. "Would you?"

Ross chuckled. "Is that supposed to be a trick question? Two years ago I would have loved it. Now, well, I'm a one-woman man. You will be, too, Linc. One of these days before you get too old to make love to a woman."

Linc rose from his chair and walked over

to one of the posts supporting the roof over the porch. Propping his shoulder against it, he gazed across the mountain top to the big ranch house where his father had once lived with his mother.

"You don't know what you're talking about, Ross. That sort of thing doesn't interest me at all. Never has and never will. You know that."

"No. I don't know anything of the kind. What I do see is a man who's missing a hell of a lot of living. And I've never understood why."

Glancing over his shoulder at Ross, he said, "Is that what you come up here for? To give me some sort of mental therapy? If it was, then you can just get the hell back down the mountain. I don't need it."

"Why no. It sounds like you're in a wonderful frame of mind," Ross said with sarcasm, then shook his head in a helpless fashion. "I thought Nevada would have already brought you out of this funk you're in, but I can see she hasn't made any headway. Poor woman, she'll probably be ripping those bandages off you way ahead of time if you keep this up."

Linc started to bark back at him, then shut his mouth as he realized he'd be adding fodder to Ross's assessment of him. Jerking the brim of his hat down on his forehead, he asked, "Did you get that supplement for the horses yesterday? I don't want any of the gestating mares to go without."

"Yeah. I got it. Twenty sacks. It was all the feed store had."

"Has Skinny been sitting up nights with Miss Lori?"

"Yeah. He's wearing himself out, too."

Skinny was the oldest wrangler on the T Bar K and, except for Marina, had worked for the ranch longer than anyone. Linc realized the man was heading toward his upper seventies and needed his rest. But there wasn't anyone, other than himself, that he would trust with the young mare.

"You think I don't know that?" Linc retorted the question. "But what the hell am I supposed to do about it? There's an eighty-percent chance she'll foal in the dark. Other than a vet, there's no one besides Skinny that I would want around in case something goes wrong. She's young and this is her first foal. He'll know what to watch for."

Sighing heavily, Ross rose to his feet and walked over to where Linc continued to slump against the porch post.

"Look, Linc, I realize you miss the horses—"

"Do you?" Linc interrupted roughly, then murmured in an easier voice, "I doubt you understand how much. They're my life."

Ross didn't say anything for a few moments and then he gently placed his hand on Linc's shoulder.

"Maybe this is a good time to think about that."

Surprised that his cousin would make such a remark, Linc looked around, but by then Ross was already stepping down from the porch and walking to his truck.

"I'll see you tomorrow," he called over his shoulder.

As Ross turned the vehicle around to

head back down the mountain, Linc lifted his hand in a farewell gesture, while desperately wishing he was going down to the ranch yard with his cousin. By this time of morning the place would be quiet. But just after daybreak, the barns and corrals were always buzzing with cowboys spreading feed, catching horses from the remuda and saddling up for the day's work.

Batwing chaps and fringed chinks would slap against jeans-covered legs. Spurs would jingle and sweat-stained felt would shade every eye. Flying horse hair and dust would fill the air and mingle with the lingering smells of breakfast from the bunkhouse.

That was the time of day he loved the most, Linc thought. When everything was starting all fresh and new and he would walk from one end of the horse barn to the other, greeting each velvety nose and big trusting eye with a stroke of his hand and a gentle word.

It was a life that he loved with every fiber of his being. And though Ross pretended to understand his feelings about the matter, his cousin didn't really know the depth of Linc's devotion to the ranch or his horses. After all, Ross had Bella. She was the love of his life now. Not the T Bar K.

By the time lunch rolled around Nevada was still full of the breakfast she'd consumed. But she prepared Linc a bowl of vegetable soup and a hefty beef sandwich and called him into the house.

While he ate she made herself busy in another part of the house. But when she heard him making his way outside to the porch again, she emerged from her bedroom and intercepted him at the front door.

"Don't bother going out and sitting down on the porch again," she said. "You've already done that enough for today."

He glared at her. "You might be my nurse, Nevada, but you're not about to tell me where to sit and how often."

Feeling a little testy herself, she punched his chest with her forefinger. "You got the first part right, partner. I'm your nurse and you're to follow my orders. You're not a sick man, you just can't use your hands. Yet." She drew in a deep breath and stepped back from him. "And if you ever expect to go back to work, you need to get a little exercise."

The corner of his lip curled upward as his gaze swept over her with a pointed look. "I'm sure a girl like you knows just the sort of exercise I need."

A girl like her. Linc Ketchum didn't know anything about the intimate part of her life. It was beyond her where or why he'd gotten the idea that she was a floozy or something worse. As far as she was concerned, having male friends wasn't decaying her morals. But she wasn't about to start defending or explaining herself to this man. Let him think what he wanted. She would be gone from here soon and he could shoot his moody, cutting remarks at someone else.

"As a matter of fact, I do."

His brows formed a dark line as she looped her arm through his and urged him out the door.

"What are you doing now?" he asked.

"We're going for a walk."

"A walk! Like hell. We're not two kids getting off the school bus and you don't have an armload of books to carry, so you can go for your own walk and leave me alone."

She pursed her lips with disapproval. "So you can sit here and get soft and flabby? I promised Dr. Olstead—"

"Oh, all right, all right," he conceded. "Let's go. But I can tell you right now that it's silly. A man doesn't walk. Not when he can ride a horse or drive a truck."

"Neither of which you can do at the moment," she pointed out sweetly.

"You like reminding me of that, don't you?"

Her expression sobered as she urged him down the steps. "I don't need to remind you of your injuries. You already feel sorry enough for yourself without that."

Stepping onto the ground, Linc halted and stared at her. "Sorry for myself? In my entire life I've never felt sorry for myself."

"Is that so?"

"Yeah. That's so."

"Hmm. A few minutes ago, in the kitchen, I could hear you raising your voice to Ross out here on the porch. Is that the way you normally talk to him?"

Linc's lips compressed in a tight line. "No. But—"

"You're frustrated because you can't go to work with him. Right?"

"That's right," he clipped. And he was also frustrated because each time he looked upon her face he wanted to touch it with his lips, to taste her sweetness over and over. But that wasn't her fault. Neither was it her fault that he had these damned bandages wrapped around his arms and hands. He needed to quit taking his aggravation out on anyone who crossed his path. Especially this woman, who was only here to help him. If his father could see him now, he'd be ashamed of his son's behavior. Linc was even ashamed of it.

"Is it helping matters to be so angry?" she asked.

A sheepish expression crept over his face before he finally shook his head. "Sorry, Nevada. It seems like all I've been doing since you got here is growling and then trying to apologize. I don't really feel sorry for myself. I understand I'll be well in a few days. And I'm damned thankful for that. But—"

Rather than finish his sentence, he curled his bandaged fingers around her arm and urged her forward. As Nevada walked along beside him, she waited for him to continue. When he didn't add anything else to his remarks, she said, "You're thankful. But. But what?"

Heaving out a breath, he lifted his face to the sky. Gray clouds were beginning to drift across the western sky and Linc carefully surveyed them. Normally the afternoon lightning storms didn't begin until July. The sky should remain calm until the two of them returned to the house.

His gaze returned to her face. "You really want to know?"

Nodding, she said, "That's why I asked."

Shrugging, he halted their forward movement. "All right, Nevada, I'm going to be honest with you. I hate like hell being unable to work and care for myself. But that's not what's really bothering me. You are."

Nevada shouldn't have been surprised by his comment. Not after the episode that had occurred between them in the kitchen this morning. Still, she had not expected him to be so open and direct with her and it shook her more than she cared to admit.

"I'm sorry," she said in a strained whisper. And she meant it. In spite of Linc's gruff rudeness, she liked him. She respected all the things he'd done with his life and the standards he'd set for himself. "I honestly don't want to cause you any more problems than you already have."

For a moment he closed his eyes and Nevada used the time to study the firm line of his lips, to remember and relish those seconds he had kissed her so passionately. She'd never felt anything like it before and though she was smart enough not to repeat the act, she was aching to tilt her face up to his, to invite his lips back down to hers.

"Nevada, I know that I've been behaving like an ass to you. And I wouldn't blame you if you walked off and told Victoria she had a monster for a cousin."

He glanced away from her and for the first time since she'd met Linc Ketchum she believed she was seeing the real man and not the growling bear who'd been doing his best to scare her away. There was regret on his face and something else that looked like raw need.

Carefully, she touched his arm at a spot above the bandaged area. "There's no need for you to be so hard on yourself, Linc. I understand. I really do," she said softly.

He groaned. "You're so young. How could you?"

She swallowed hard as his dark-green eyes met hers. "Because when you kissed me I was afraid."

A mixture of disbelief and regret washed over his face as he reached out and touched her cheek. "Nevada, I never meant to scare you. I can't even remember the last time I kissed a woman. I guess I've forgotten how to treat one."

Shaking her head, she turned her back to him and drew in a deep breath. "You didn't scare me, Linc. Not in the way you're thinking. I was scared because I liked it—a lot."

For long moments the silence was only broken by the breeze whispering through the pines and the chatter of a nearby magpie to its mate. Nevada could only wonder what the man was thinking. Probably that she was truly a promiscuous woman. Well, it didn't matter, she told herself. All that mattered was that he get well and that she leave this ranch with her senses and her heart intact.

"I liked it, too."

The gentle tone of his voice shocked her even more than his words and she dared to look over her shoulder at him.

"But it isn't going to happen again," she stated with certainty.

"No. I don't have any interest in having

a relationship with a woman. And I'm sure you have plans of your own," he said.

Not serious plans, she thought. Not with any certain man. But she didn't explain any of that to him. He didn't care about her plans. He was just trying to get through the next couple of weeks with a nurse in his house.

"Sure," she murmured, then trying not to feel so deflated, she gave him a wry smile. "Ready to walk now? I realize you don't want to, but it will be good for you. And I'd like to see more of the place. Are there any trails around here that we might follow?"

With a faint look of relief on his face, he nodded. "There used to be one that led away from the back of the house. It's rough, but the view is pretty."

"Good," she said cheerfully. "Let's go."

Linc glanced down at her feet. The strapped sandals she'd been wearing earlier had been replaced with a pair of black cowboy boots and he looked at her with faint surprise.

"You're wearing cowboy boots."

She chuckled. "Sure. I may not be a cowgirl, but I enjoy Western fashion. And this pair is good to walk in. They have treads on the bottom of the soles."

"So they do," he said with a faint smile, then gently urged her in the direction of the trail.

The track Linc recalled had become so overgrown that it took them a few minutes to find it. But finally they discovered a faint rut covered with pine needles and decaying cottonwood leaves. For several yards the track was mostly on level ground and wound gently through a thick stand of trees and scattered boulders. Then the landscape changed abruptly and they began a slippery descent down the side of the mountain.

"Are you sure you want to continue?" Linc asked as she followed closely behind his lead. "This is getting rough and is likely to get worse the farther we go. Looks like the rains have created some treacherous gullies."

Small stones and loose gravel had already caused Nevada to slip more than once, but she wasn't about to turn around and go back. The view around them was becoming more and more spectacular.

"I'm not worried," she assured him, then asked, "How far does this trail go?"

"I haven't been down it in years, but if I remember right the path goes all the way to a meadow. About three-quarters of the way down there's a spot where I always stopped before I ever reached the meadow. I used to go there as a kid to be by myself."

Nevada took her gaze off the trail long enough to allow herself a glimpse of his wide, rugged back and long, strong legs. What had he been like as a young boy, she wondered. Surely his father's death had affected him deeply. But a death in the family was something that couldn't be helped. According to Marina, Darla Ketchum had chosen to leave her son behind. That was a different matter altogether.

"Sounds as though you've never been a social person," she said.

"Not really. I like people. But I like my own company, too."

"I can see that you're nothing like your cousin Ross. I never had the chance to meet his brother Hugh before he was killed. And I've only met Seth a couple of times. Are you like either one of them?"

Linc shook his head. "Maybe a little like Hugh. He was a quiet homebody."

But even in his short life Hugh had had a wife and child, Nevada thought. Except for his cousins, Linc didn't appear to have any immediate family. And as for him bunking with the ranch hands, that wasn't exactly Nevada's idea of having a home.

He glanced over his shoulder at her. "What about you, Nevada? You don't have any siblings either?"

She shook her head. "No. My mother had some sort of medical problem after she gave birth to me. It prevented her from having more children. I would've loved to have had a brother or sister. It's lonely being the only one. But, well, my mother is the sort who didn't need more children. I'm not sure she even needed me," she added glumly.

Linc paused on the steep trail and she stopped as he stood there looking at her. "That's a bad thing to say."

"Not really. I'm only being realistic. You see, as I told you before, my mother had lots of problems with my dad. He wasn't the nicest man in the world." She looked away and found that she was a bit embarrassed to be admitting such things to this man. Talking about her parents with anyone, even people that she'd been acquainted with for a long time, was difficult. "He abused her in more ways than one."

Sadness tinged Linc's eyes. "I'm sorry about that, Nevada."

Shrugging, she glanced his way. "Me too. But that was a long time ago and I try not to let it bother me now. He went his way and my mother's gone hers. At least there's no more fighting and yelling and cheating and threatening. I would never—"

Her expression turned grim as her words trailed away.

"Never what?" Linc prodded, surprised to find himself interested in the facts about her life.

She shrugged again. "Nothing," she said with a wan smile. "Just that I'd never want to live through it again."

Linc nodded marginally and then turned and started walking on down the trail. While he plodded forward, he couldn't help thinking about his own parents and how much a part of Nevada's story matched his own.

He could still hear his mother yelling threats and demands at his father and even now when a woman raised her voice in Linc's presence, it made him cringe with memories. There was no way he would ever want to put himself or a child of his through such misery.

"I understand."

"Do you?" she asked. "I can't imagine. You've been raised in a nice family."

"Even nice families have their problems, Nevada."

Nevada was wondering what he meant

by that comment when the forest around them opened up and the trail they were traveling narrowed down to a rocky path on the edge of a steep bluff.

Linc halted his forward motion and turned to her. "This ground is so washed out here that I'm not sure we should go on."

Nevada looked around her. To their left was a small copse of fir trees, fallen tree trunks and moss-covered boulders. To their immediate right, where the bluff fell away, there was nothing but open air, and at least a hundred-foot drop to the next shelf of the mountain. "Is this the place you used to visit?" she asked.

"No. It's still a bit farther on." Moving toward her, he took by the arm. "Come on. I think we should turn around."

"But I want to see. And I won't fall," she assured him. "I'm as sure-footed as a mule."

Wary, Linc shook his head. "That has to be the craziest thing I've ever heard. I'm supposed to be a patient. And you're the nurse. What are we doing out here mountain-climbing?"

She grinned at him. "Are you tired?"

"No. Not in the least. But—"

"I'm the nurse and I'm making sure that you're getting your exercise. And from what I can see you haven't gotten enough yet," she said impishly.

Before Linc realized what he was doing, a chuckle rumbled up from his chest. "Are you always like this?" he asked.

"Like what?"

The corners of his eyes crinkled with amusement. "Are you always so chipper and adventurous. And happy?"

It was such a joy to hear him laugh and see him smile that Nevada felt as though she was standing on bubbly water instead of rocky ground.

"Usually. It's much more fun than being angry and sad." The afternoon had grown hot and Nevada used the back of her forearm to wipe at the perspiration that dotted her forehead. "Have you ever been happy, Linc?"

He laughed again and Nevada realized she could get addicted to the pleasant sound. It was low and as roughly masculine as the tough brown whiskers on his face.

"You mean, you wonder if I've always been a sulky bastard?"

Her smile was shy and totally enchanting to Linc and he suddenly realized it felt good to be walking in the woods with Nevada. He'd not ever done such a thing with a woman and this excursion was turning out to be far more pleasant than he'd ever expected.

"I didn't use those words. You did," she reminded him.

He shrugged and glanced away from her as the reality of his life begin to edge its way back into his thoughts. He wasn't sure he knew what being happy was. But one thing he did understand, he wasn't the badgered, broken man his father had been.

"I'm mostly happy, Nevada. And that's all a man can hope to be."

A brief smile touched her lips. "Well, I guess that's all a woman can hope to be, too." She stepped forward and carefully took hold of his bandaged hand. "You know what, I'd be even happier if you'd lead me on down the mountain. I want to see where you used to sit and dream as a boy."

He could feel something warm tugging at his insides and he realized he was glad that she'd shaken him out of his dark mood, that the two of them had made a sort of peace between them.

"All right. We'll go on down. Just hold onto my hand. I don't want you to fall," he told her.

Nevada shook her head regretfully. "I can't. If I slipped you'd try to grab me and that wouldn't be good for the new skin forming over your fingers. But don't worry about me. Like I said—"

"You're a surefooted as a mule," he interrupted. "And just about as independent." Turning his back to her, he motioned toward the center of his belt. "Hold onto to my belt loops. And don't argue. The next few feet down are a little scary."

Nevada latched her fingers through the loops of his jeans, while thinking nothing could be as frightening as the strange emotions that were beginning to rush over her like a sudden burst of hot sunshine.

Linc Ketchum was her patient. She wasn't supposed to be feeling anything toward the man except concern for his physical well-being. But everything about him mesmerized her and she could only wonder how long it would be before he totally captivated her heart.

Chapter Eight

Linc hadn't been kidding about the trail turning treacherous. The path was nothing more than a narrow, winding ledge. In several places the earth had washed away to leave gaping cracks. If Nevada allowed herself to look she could see the distant, rocky ground below. But she tried not to look at the danger and simply focused on putting one foot safely in front of the other.

More than once during their downward descent, Nevada desperately wanted to grab on to Linc's waist and hold on for dear life. But she figured he would resent that intimate sort of contact. And after the fragile truce they'd made, she didn't want to have him thinking she was deliberately trying to stir the ashes left behind by the hot kiss they'd shared.

Thankfully, the trail suddenly widened and then they were stepping down onto a wide ledge of solid rock. The sound of tinkling water immediately caught Nevada's attention and she looked to her far left to see a small waterfall pouring over a rim of red rock. About ten feet below, the crystal-clear water pooled in a large dished-out spot that was framed with rocks and dead wood.

"Oh! How absolutely beautiful!" Nevada exclaimed. "Where is the water coming from? The snow melt is over for this summer."

He pointed upward to a crease in the mountain. "There's a natural spring up there. As far as I know it's never gone dry."

Totally enchanted, Nevada released her safety hold on his belt loops and walked closer to the waterfall.

"I don't know much about the outdoors, but it must be unusual to find a spring in this arid climate. We're not totally desert here by any means, but we're not living in a tropical zone either."

Linc walked up beside her. "You're right. I think it is an oddity. On all the thousands of acres on this ranch, I've never discovered another one."

She tilted her head to look up at him and there was a sparkle of pleasure in her eyes that made Linc's stomach do a funny little turn.

"This is just wonderful, Linc," Nevada went on. "Thank you for bringing me here." She glanced around for a place to sit down. "Would it be okay if we rested a few minutes before we start back? I'm not as much of a mountain goat as I thought."

"Sure. Just don't get too close to the edge of the bluff. It's a long drop over. I doubt anything could survive it. Not even a mountain goat."

A few feet away, a fallen log rested near the wall of mountain. Linc gestured toward it. "Let's sit here."

She nodded at his suggestion and the two

of them found a comfortable seat on the dead pine trunk.

Nevada sighed with pleasure as she stretched her legs out in front of her and wiped once again at the sweat trickling at her temples.

"I never dreamed there would be a place like this around here," she said as she gazed at the splendorous view before them. "You can see the meadow from here. And there's some of your Angus grazing down there. Is there a chance that we'll see any of your horses down there with them?" she asked.

Linc pushed the black hat he was wearing to the back of his head. "No. We do have part of the remuda pastured now, but they're in a different section of the ranch."

"How big is the remuda?" she asked curiously.

"I think we have about two hundred and ten horses now."

"Wow. That's a lot."

"Quite a few," he agreed. "And that doesn't include the broodmares and colts."

"Why so many?" she asked, then shot

him an apologetic look. "Sorry, Linc. I'm sure my questions sound naive. I'm not very educated about ranching, but I find it interesting."

His gaze rested on her face and for a second Nevada thought she spotted a bit of surprise on his face. But then he looked away from her and she lost the chance to gauge his expression.

"We have so many horses," he answered, "because the T Bar K does everything just as it was done sixty, sixty-five years ago. You won't find helicopters or four-wheelers taking the place of horses here. Our cowboys do all the cutting and roundups on horseback. It's a tradition that will never change as long as a Ketchum is breathing."

His statement told her a lot about his feelings for the ranch and how much his heritage and place in it meant to him. It was a trait she admired. Most of the men she came in contact with weren't interested in their past or where their roots originated. But then, some of them were like her; their roots were rotten.

"Tell me about this place," she urged. "How did it get started?"

He looked at her once more and this time she could see faint skepticism pulling his brows together.

"You really want to know?" he asked.

"Sure. Why wouldn't I?" she asked with a puzzled frown. "The T Bar K is known far and wide. But I've never actually heard its history."

Maybe she was truly interested, Linc thought. Or maybe she was only pretending to be just to butter him up a bit.

Hell, Linc, why would she want to do that? She doesn't want anything from you. And she sure didn't need to patronize him just to get his attention. All she had to do was button his shirt and he melted like a snowflake on a hot tongue.

"Well, it began with my father, Randolf, and his brother Tucker. They were both born in Texas and raised there. Their father, Nate, was a big cattleman and he owned a ranch near Goliad that had been handed down to him through generations of Ketchums. It was prime land and worth a fortune."

Already enthralled by the story, Nevada said, "Oh. So why did they come up here to New Mexico?"

He shook his head at her with faint amusement. "I thought nurses were supposed to be patient creatures."

"All right. Go on. I won't interrupt with questions," she promised.

"My cousins and I have heard lots of tales from our fathers. But we're not really sure if it was the way things really happened back then. All of us believe they didn't want us to know the entire truth of the matter."

"Hmm. Why do you think that?"

Linc dangled his bandaged hands between his knees as he stared off into the distance. "We're not sure. Except that we believe something scandalous happened. But that would be after Nate got into financial trouble and began to sell off blocks of land. That was during the Depression and the land didn't sell for much. Randolf and

Tucker were just young boys then, but they recalled the hard times. Eventually though, Nate pulled things together somehow and after the war started, cattle were in demand again. He began to make piles of money and he bought back the land he'd sold."

"Well, that sounds like everything began to get better," Nevada remarked.

"I guess it got too good," he said with a wry grimace. "You know, the more money a man has, the more troubles he seems to acquire. Anyway—and here's where the story gets sketchy—our grandmother, Sarah, caught Granddad cheating with another woman. And—"

"Cheating! But weren't they old by then?" Nevada interrupted.

"I guess some men never get too old to have a roaming eye. Anyway that was when the trouble started brewing. Eventually Sarah demanded a divorce and her half of the cattle empire."

"Let me guess," Nevada replied. "Nate refused."

Linc nodded. "I think the ranch turned

into a hellish place after that. Our grandfather wound up being murdered. He'd been shot and his body thrown into a thick patch of weesatche."

Nevada was shocked. "Oh no. What happened? Do you know?"

Linc shook his head. "Not really. People down there believed Sarah shot him and had her lover hide the body."

By now Nevada was incredulous. "She had a lover too?"

His expression turned to disgust. "Yeah. For spite, I guess. Isn't it nice to hear you come from such a loving family?" he asked sarcastically.

So Linc's parents hadn't been the only ones with marriage problems, Nevada decided. No wonder he had a bad view of relationships between men and women. He must think that all marriages were flawed and painful as those of his grandparents and his own parents had been.

She wanted to tell him that nothing could be further from the truth. There were married people who truly loved each other, who would die for each other. All he had to do was take a look at his cousins. But she didn't say anything. It would be hypocritical of her when she'd made a promise to herself always to be a free and independent woman.

"What happened to Sarah? Was she charged for his death?"

"No. Seems there wasn't enough evidence. So after Nate was buried, Randolf and Tucker decided they didn't want any part of the ranch. They told Sarah to keep it and good riddance."

Nevada shook her head sadly. "They believed she murdered their father."

This time Linc was the one who looked surprised. "Well, don't you?"

"How could I know that without hearing all the facts? It's not good for a person to jump to conclusions too quickly. You might turn out to be wrong."

"I've been wrong before and it didn't kill me. Better to be wrong about a person than dead. If Noah Rider could talk to us, I'm sure he'd agree with that."

Noah Rider was the old foreman who'd been murdered on T Bar K land about two years ago. His body had been discovered in a dry arroyo several miles away from the ranch house. The incident had garnered interest far and wide and Victoria's husband, Jess, had nearly died from a gunshot wound received while investigating the crime. Nevada could remember what a trying time it had been for the whole Ketchum family. But it sounded as though trouble was not something new to this clan.

"So your dad and uncle came up here and started this ranch," Nevada mused aloud. "Where did they get the money to build on?"

Linc shook his head ever so slightly as he peered into the hazy distance. "Well, that's another place where the story gets a little foggy. My dad always told me that he and his brother got their grubstake from their mother. You see, her family had owned lots of oil rights and she'd given her two sons part of the royalties. But Tucker always told a different version. He said that the money they'd used to start the T Bar K had belonged to Nate and when they'd left Texas they'd taken a share of their father's estate."

"How odd that they would tell the story so differently," Nevada commented. "Which one did you believe more? Your father?"

Linc nodded. "Not just because he was my father," he explained. "But Tucker tended to exaggerate the facts at times. And anyway, after all these years it doesn't matter. They made the ranch go and we children are still here keeping their legacy going."

Nevada was fascinated by the story, and as she sat there mulling over everything he'd told her, she realized there were plenty more questions she would have liked to ask about his family. Especially about his mother. What part had she played in all of this? Had she come from Texas, too?

Deciding she didn't want to take the chance on ruining the peace between them, she kept the questions to herself. If Linc ever wanted to talk to her about his mother, he would have to bring up the subject himself.

She looked over to see Linc suddenly squinting up at the sky and she followed his example. Dark-gray clouds were beginning to swirl and mix above them.

"Are those rain clouds?" Nevada asked. "If they are, we're in trouble. It will take us half an hour to get back to the house."

Linc continued to study the skyline. "I think we're in trouble. And I'm not sure if we should try to head back right now. Or wait it out here where we might have shelter."

"Shelter?" Nevada looked around her. Except for one lone juniper jutting out from a crack in the rocks, she didn't see anything that would shield them from lightning and rain. "I don't see any kind of protection around here."

Rising to his feet, Linc pointed toward the waterfall. "That's one of the things that always fascinated me about this place. Have you ever seen one of those old movies where the bandits ride beneath the waterfall and enter a hideout cave?"

Nevada nodded. "Sure. Hasn't everyone? But don't tell me there's a cave behind this waterfall. That's just too much to believe."

He took her by the arm. "Come on. I'll show you."

Nevada pulled back. "Linc! We'll get wet. Your bandages will get soaked and that would be bad. Let's head to the house."

He started to say something when a loud crack split the air around them and rumbled down the mountainside.

Nevada jumped back to the safety of Linc's side and instinctively clutched his upper arm. "What are we going to do? I don't relish getting fried by lightning."

"Neither do I," he said. "I've already had my share of frying." He looked down at her. "I don't think we have much of a choice. Either way the waterfall or the rain is going to get us wet. At least in the cave we'll be protected from the lightning."

Nevada nodded as another bolt of electricity sizzled through the air and struck a nearby tree. A ball of fire raced up the trunk and Linc quickly tugged on her hand.

"Come on!"

Nevada didn't make any protest as they raced toward the fall of water.

"Duck your head," he warned. "The cave is small."

She did as he instructed and the two of them leaped through the icy flow of water. Once past, Nevada could see they were standing in a natural indentation of the rock. The opening was no more than four feet by six, but it was dry and cozy and would protect them from the violent lightning that was so deadly in this part of the West.

"Not a vacation suite, but at least it's dry," Linc said as the two of them moved toward the back of the enclosure.

"Thank God it's here," Nevada exclaimed. "And I would never have believed it if you hadn't shown me."

"Let's sit down," he suggested. "This might last for a while."

There was just enough room for the two

of them to sit side by side with their knees drawn toward them. As Nevada wiped at the water droplets on her hair, she said, "I'm sorry about this, Linc. When I asked you to take a walk, I didn't know it was going to turn into this much of an outing."

"Forget it. And anyway, it's better than being cooped in the house or planted on the porch."

"I know. But it would be awful for you to survive such a horrible fire and then be killed because your nurse had you out in an electrical storm. Lord, I'd never get a job after that."

He looked at her with amusement. "You think Victoria would fire you if that happened?"

"No doubt," Nevada said grimly. "You're her hero."

Linc didn't make any sort of reply to that. Compliments of any sort made him feel awkward and he was already having enough trouble with being jammed in this tiny rock room with Nevada. Their shoulders and arms were squashed together, along with their thighs. The heat from both their bodies was already filling the small space and causing him to sweat beneath his shirt. Or maybe the desire to kiss Nevada again was making him sweat. Either way, he hoped the thunderstorm ended soon.

"It's hard to see through the waterfall. But it looks like it's raining now," Nevada said as she peered intently forward.

A part of Linc's gaze was on the opening in front of them, but the other part was darting to her face, which was only inches away from his. Her rosy-tan skin was as smooth as fine spun silk and along her cheekbone there was a faint bloom of roses. Black hair curled in tiny ringlets against her ear and temple, then fell in shiny waves upon her shoulder.

She was a naturally gorgeous woman and he tried to convince himself that her beauty was the reason he wanted to kiss her, touch her in forbidden places.

Stifling back a groan of desperation, he said, "It's pouring. I can hear it."

Her gaze carefully searched the fall of

water a few short feet in front of them, then turned up to his face. "Really?"

He opened his mouth to answer at the same time another crack of lightning hit something outside the cave. Thunder rocked the mountainside like the after-shocks of an explosion. Before Nevada re-alized what she was doing, she screamed and turned her face into Linc's shoulder.

"Oh God, Linc, we're going to be killed!" she wailed.

Instinctively, Linc's arms curled around her and pressed her head tightly against him. "Sssh. Don't be frightened. It's just noise. The lightning can't get us in here," he said gently.

"Are you sure?" She tilted her head back to peek up at him. "We're sitting on rock! And there's water right in front of us!"

"Yes, but at least we're not targets here like we would be outside. Don't think about the worst happening. Just tell yourself it will all be over in a few minutes."

Before she could make any sort of reply another network of lightning streaked the sky and exploded somewhere outside the cave above their heads.

Nevada buried her face in his shoulder and as Linc gazed down at the top of her head, he realized he didn't know the first thing about calming a frightened woman. The brief times he'd spent in the company of a female hadn't involved situations like this.

But he figured Nevada was no different than a nervous filly that needed a gentle hand on her, so he began to stroke his fingers softly down the black mane of hair resting against her back.

"Don't be scared, little one," he murmured against her temple. "I'm not going to let anything happen to you."

Nevada wasn't usually afraid of electrical storms. The afternoon light shows were a common occurrence in this part of the country. But she'd never been caught out of doors in one before. And certainly not in the mountains where everything was more of a target.

But she trusted Linc to keep them safe

and the security of his arms was having a steadying affect on her jumpy nerves. The warmth of his body soothed her while his unique male scent was slowly seducing her senses.

After a few moments she began to forget about the sizzling streaks of lightning and ear-shattering thunder. Being this close to Linc was doing all sorts of things to her body and she realized she desperately wanted to lift her face from his shoulder and turn her lips up to his.

But they'd both vowed to keep their relationship one of patient and nurse. She had to keep her side of the promise, no matter how much she wanted to break it.

Finally, she heard Linc whispering close to her ear, "I think it's letting up now."

Stirring in his arms, she lifted her head and stared toward the front of the cave. From what she could see through the wall of the waterfall, the sky was beginning to lighten. It was time to extract herself from Linc's embrace.

"Uh—it looks like the worst is over. I

guess we need to get out of here," she said as she dared to glance up at him.

The moment she lifted her face their eyes collided. Her stomach lurched wildly and her heart began to hammer.

"Yeah—I guess we do," he said in a low voice.

Nevada licked her lips and his gaze settled on them.

"I'm sorry I behaved like such a chicken." But she wasn't sorry that she was here in his arms, her body pressed close to his. It felt like the perfect place for her to be and it was all she could do to keep from sliding her arms around his neck and pressing her cheek against his.

"A person would be crazy not to fear lightning. Don't feel badly because you got a little jumpy." A wry smile twisted his lips as he brought his bandaged hand alongside her face. "Are you okay now? Feel like hiking back home?"

Home. Suddenly that word held a whole new meaning to Nevada. She'd never felt as though she'd had a real home but with

Linc she was beginning to imagine what one might be like and the pleasant thought scared her more than she cared to admit.

"Sure. Just let me get on my feet."

"Wait. I'll help you," he said and before she could make a move, he rose to his feet and reached down for her hand.

Nevada shook her head. "Linc, you're forgetting. No pressure on your hands."

"Damn it, for one minute forget about my burns and let me help you," he ordered.

She did as he asked, but she didn't allow him to pull on her weight any more than necessary. Once on her feet, she started to step around him and dash through the waterfall to the outside. But his hand on her waist prevented her from moving.

Darting a glance up at him, she tried not to notice that the two of them were face to face and hip to hip. "Thank you," she said. "For making me not feel so scared."

A faint smile tugged at the corners of his lips. "Thank you for making me come on this walk. It made me realize there's nothing wrong with me that a few days won't cure."

She smiled up at him. "Then I guess we've both made each other feel better."

His hand moved slightly up and down against her rib cage and Nevada was sure the small cave had suddenly lost all its oxygen.

"Uh—we'd better go," she said suddenly.

His hand tightened on her waist and for long moments as Nevada watched his eyes darken and his nostrils flare, she became aware that he wanted to kiss her just as badly as she wanted to kiss him. The realization caused her heart to flutter wildly in her throat and she unconsciously reached out and placed her palms against his chest.

"Nevada—I—"

"What?"

Shaking his head, he removed his hand from her waist and took hold of her arm. "Nothing," he answered grimly. "Let's get out of here before I do something stupid."

He urged her forward and Nevada followed him through the waterfall and back outside onto the ledge of rock. Everything was wet around them, but the sun was beginning to peek through the clouds.

"Look, Linc," Nevada said as she studied the rain-washed sky. "There's a rainbow over our heads. Isn't it beautiful?" She glanced over at him and smiled. "Did you know a rainbow is a promise of good things to come?"

"I always thought it meant that people foolishly chased after things they couldn't have."

"Oh, what a cynic," she said with a playful groan. "Don't you believe in just a little bit of magic?"

Normally Linc would have been quick to spit out the word *no*. But that was before he'd held Nevada in his arms. That was before he'd tasted her lips and felt himself going to a magical place where nothing mattered but making love to her.

Impatient with his soppy thoughts, he nudged her shoulder toward the now-muddy trail. "I believe we'd better get back home before Marina comes up with our supper and has a spell because she can't find us."

The pleasure at spotting the rainbow quickly fell from her face, and she hurried ahead of him to begin the steep climb up the mountain.

Behind her, Linc hated himself for being such a coward. Hated himself for not being able to run after her and admit how much he wanted to make love to her. But the memory of his mother walking away and never looking back was enough to make him keep his place safely behind her.

Chapter Nine

For the next three days Nevada and Linc settled into somewhat of a routine. He'd fixed the problem of showering by having one of the ranch hands come up and help him deal with the task. That usually took away the need for Nevada to help him dress in the mornings. Afterwards she prepared their breakfast and in the evenings, she changed his bandages and urged him to take some sort of exercise.

The walks he took were simple jaunts down the road and back to the house. Nevada never offered to go with him, and he never invited her. Which was probably for the best. Both of them were trying their best to put on an act of indifference, and it was beginning to take its toll.

At night, after the supper that Marina always brought up to them, they would go their separate ways until it was time for bed and then the provocative ordeal of undressing him would have to be gone through all over again.

Nevada's nerves were wearing thin. She'd read more novels than she'd ever read, and the idea of having a television to watch was actually becoming attractive to her.

As for Linc, she wasn't sure how he'd been spending his time. Sometimes she could hear him out on the front porch talking with Ross or some other ranch hand. The last couple of days an old buckaroo named Skinny had come up to visit him.

The first day the older man had arrived, Linc had called Nevada out on the porch to meet him. Which had surprised her somewhat. Several ranch hands had come and gone from the place in the past couple of days and he had not bothered to introduce her to any of them. The fact that he'd wanted her to meet Skinny told her the old man was important to him. And she'd found out that she liked him. He'd had a kind twinkle in his faded blue eyes and it was obvious that he adored Linc.

As for herself, Nevada had almost stopped trying to fool herself. She adored Linc, too. Only she was smart enough to keep her feelings to herself.

The ring of the telephone punctured Nevada's thoughts and she left her seat in the living room to hurry to the kitchen to answer it.

"Nevada, it's Victoria. I'm down here at the big ranch house and I thought I might run up to see you for a few minutes. Are you busy?"

Nevada laughed lightly. "Busy? What would I be doing? It's like a tomb around here."

"Poor thing. I'll bet you're about to go out of your mind."

"Not exactly," Nevada hedged.

"Well, you can tell me all about it in a few minutes. And I've got an appointment card for Linc. Dr. Olstead wants to see him tomorrow at eleven."

"You're just full of news," Nevada remarked, then asked, "Are the babies with you?"

"Brace yourself," Victoria laughed. "I have both of them with me. Better get Linc some earplugs before I get there."

She hung up and Nevada walked through the house in search of her patient.

After a quick peek on the porch and the back patio, she finally found him in his bedroom reading a hardbound book. He was propped against the headboard with a couple of pillows cushioning his back. Heedless of the fancy coverlet, his brown cowboy boots were crossed at the ankles and Nevada could only think it was a good thing he hadn't been walking around in the feed lot.

Since the door was fully open, she knocked lightly on the facing. "Sorry to disturb you, Linc, but that was Victoria who just called. She's coming up to see you—us."

He stood on the floor and with a puzzled frown glanced at his wristwatch. "It's the middle of the afternoon. What's she doing off work?"

"I didn't ask. She probably had Dr. Martinez take her place today. I'll go make coffee before she gets here."

Nevada left him and hurried to the kitchen to put a few refreshments together. The coffeepot was almost full and Marina's famous cowboy cookies were laid out on a tray when Nevada heard Victoria's vehicle arrive in front of the house. As she walked to the front door to greet her boss and friend, she could hear Katrina and little Sam both squealing with loud delight.

Stepping onto the porch, she could see that Linc had already met the little group and had somehow managed to lift Sam up on his back. Katrina was hopping eagerly at his side.

"I wanta ride too, Uncle Linc. Let me ride, too," she pleaded.

"Uncle Linc can't give you a ride now," Victoria told her daughter as the little group headed to the house. "He shouldn't even be carrying Sam. You run on ahead and find Aunt Nevada."

Nevada used that cue to step from the

porch and call to the little girl. "Here, Katrina!"

With a loud squeal of excitement, Katrina raced to Nevada and jumped straight into her arms.

Laughing, Nevada lifted the three-and-a-half-year-old high in the air, then set her back on her feet and smacked a big kiss on her cheek.

"Hi, Aunt Nevada! You smell good! And you look pretty, too. Do you think I look pretty? Mommy bought me a new dress." Lifting the pink skirt on both sides, the golden-haired child twirled around on her toes for Nevada.

Her eyes sparkling with love, Nevada kissed the girl's cheek again. "Oh, I wish I had a dress like that. You look like the most beautiful girl in the world."

Beaming, Katrina turned to the other two adults who had reached the porch. "Mommy, Uncle Linc! Nevada says I'm the most beautiful girl in the world."

"Well, you are, aren't you?" Linc asked his niece as he bent down and allowed the dark-headed toddler on his back to step onto the porch. Sam was just over a year old but extremely steady on his feet. Linc had predicted the boy was going to make a championship bronc rider, but Victoria refused to think of her baby doing such a dangerous sport. She was even skittish when Jess rode the tot around on his gentle roping horse.

"Nope," Katrina told him. "I'm just pretty. Nevada is beautiful."

Laughing with embarrassment, Nevada reached out and playfully swatted the girl's bottom. "I think you're making up fairy tales, young lady."

While Katrina giggled and danced, Sam left Linc's side and toddled over to Nevada. Raising his arms up to her, he said, "Nada. Up, Nada!"

Bending down, Nevada lovingly scooped up the boy and cuddled him in her arms. "Come on, Sam, let's go have a cookie. Okay?"

"'Kay!" he shouted with enough enthusiasm to make the adults laugh.

Nevada carried the toddler into the house while Katrina and the other two adults followed. In the kitchen, Victoria settled the children at the table with cookies and milk while Nevada poured fresh coffee for the adults.

"What are you doing off work?" Linc asked his cousin.

Victoria took a seat next to Sam. "I needed a day to get caught up on some personal chores. Dr. Martinez is filling in for me," she answered, then turned a pointed look on Nevada. "He wasn't at all happy when he found out you weren't working at the clinic. He thinks he can't do anything without you."

Nevada frowned. "You're exaggerating even more than your daughter."

"Hmmph. I think he's sweet on you. He's just too shy to say anything to you about it," Victoria remarked.

Across the room, Linc leaned his hip against the cabinet counter and watched Nevada take a seat across from his cousin. He could see a pink tinge of embarrassment on her cheeks and Linc was suddenly struck by the thought that once Nevada left here she would be fair game for any man's attention. The notion irked him, but in the same breath he tried to tell himself that her personal life was none of his business.

"Dr. Martinez is rather old for Nevada, don't you think?" he asked his cousin.

Victoria turned her attention to him. "He's not much older than you, Linc. And he's a good-looking man. If I were Nevada I'd be flattered by his attention."

"Oh, Victoria, don't be silly. I don't need you to round me up a boyfriend. I already have plenty. Besides, if I ever dated the man it would be awkward to work with him later."

"Hmm. That's true," Victoria agreed as she returned her attention to Nevada. "And you're right. You have plenty of guys waiting to date you without me scrounging you up another one. Even if he is a rich, well-to-do doctor."

"Is that what you come up here for?" Linc shot at her. "Just to talk about Nevada's boyfriends?"

Victoria was clearly surprised by Linc's outburst and her mouth fell open as she stared at him. "Is something wrong with that?"

Linc suddenly felt like an idiot and with a deep frown marring his forehead he marched over to the table and picked up a cookie from the tray.

"No," he answered without bothering to give any explanation for his remark. How could he explain his burst of jealousy, he wondered, when he didn't even understand it himself.

Victoria continued to look at him with a keen eye. "Well, actually, I didn't come up here to discuss anything with Nevada. I came to see you and to check on how you're doing. Nevada tells me you've been in a better mood, but now I'm beginning to wonder if she only told me that to appease me."

Little Sam had eaten most of his cookie and was now placing the last of the crumbs on top of his head, which was making Katrina giggle hysterically and was prompting him to keep repeating the act.

Nevada used the children's antics as a

good excuse to leave the table and take the two of them outside.

"I think we'll go pick some wildflowers," she told Victoria. "You go ahead and visit with Linc."

As Nevada hurried the two children out of the kitchen, Linc walked over to the table and sat down across from his cousin.

Victoria heaved out a disgusted sigh. "Well, you managed to run her off without much effort."

Linc lifted his bandaged hands in a gesture of helplessness. "I didn't do any such thing. And why are you suddenly badgering me?"

"Because you make me angry. I want to see my dear cousin Linc and instead you—oh, just forget it. You're just a man."

She reached into the pocket of her shirt, pulled out a small white card and placed it on the table between them.

Ignoring it, Linc asked, "What is that supposed to mean? Are you and Jess having marital problems?"

Tilting her head back, Victoria laughed.

"Not in the least. How could you even think such a thing?"

He turned a brooding expression out the window where Nevada was now romping with Sam and Katrina. "It happens," he quipped. "A lot."

"Well, not with us. Never with us. In fact, we're thinking about having another baby," Victoria admitted.

This brought his head around and he stared at her in surprise. "Another baby! But Sam isn't yet two! And you already have two children."

She shrugged as a dreamy expression crossed her face. "So we do. But there's not a limit, is there? We might want four or five or six."

Shaking his head, Linc said, "Kids are nice. But I don't understand your need for more of them. They're lots of work."

Victoria grinned at him. "So are your colts. But you wouldn't understand, Linc. Not until you have a family of your own."

He looked away from her and in spite of himself, he found his gaze drawn back to the picture Nevada was making as she knelt down to help the children pick wild-flowers.

"That won't ever happen," he said lowly.

Silent moments passed before he felt Victoria's hand resting on his arm.

"Why, Linc?" she asked softly. "You know, each month, each year that passes, I keep hoping and praying that someone will come into your life."

Emotions balled in his throat and he did his best to swallow them down before he glanced at her. "You're wasting your prayers on me. You know how I feel about things."

"No. I don't. I know you've never gotten over your mother remarrying and leaving like she did, but—"

"I don't want to talk about her, Victoria. Not now."

Sighing wearily, Victoria pushed the card toward him. "There's your appointment for tomorrow. Dr. Olstead wants to make sure you've been healing all right since you left the hospital."

His arms and hands were healing, he could have told her. But his insides had gone through some sort of trauma that he couldn't shake. Ever since he'd held Nevada in the cave, he'd felt like a different man. When he looked at her now, he didn't only want to make love to her, he also wanted to protect and cherish her. He wanted to see her smile over and over and feel her joy for life flow into him.

Linc had never felt anything like what he was feeling now and he desperately wished Dr. Olstead could heal his state of mind along with his hands.

"All right. Is Nevada going to drive me in or are you going to send up one of the hands to take me?"

His question puckered her dark brows together. "Nevada is going to take you, of course. There's not one man down on the ranch who wants to sit in a doctor's office any more than you do."

"Yeah, guess you're right about that," he said flatly, then inclined his head to the view of the yard. "Sam and Katrina obviously think Nevada is wonderful."

A fond smile crossed Victoria's face. "They call her Aunt Nevada. And she's great with them." Her expression sobered as she added, "It's such a shame that she doesn't want to become a mother. She loves children so much and she'd make such a good parent. But everyone has their own demons to deal with, I suppose."

Struck by Victoria's comments, Linc's gaze traveled back and forth between the sight of Nevada frolicking with his niece and nephew to his cousin's pensive expression.

"What woman wouldn't have demons with a laundry list like Nevada probably has," he remarked. The idea that she'd gone through men the way he did clean shirts left a heavy weight inside him. And he tried to tell himself he was being stupid. He didn't want to be the next one she put through the wringer then hung out to dry.

"Oh Linc," Victoria said with a shake of her head, "you are so—messed up if you think—"

Linc narrowed his eyes on Victoria's lovely face. "What? What were you about to say?" he demanded.

With another shake of her head, Victoria

rose to her feet and carried her empty cup to the sink. "Nothing," she told him. "If you want to know anything personal about Nevada, you'll have to ask her yourself."

And he wasn't about to do that, Linc thought. He might have slipped that once and kissed her, but since then he'd kept his distance and he had not allowed any family or personal talk to come up between them. The past three days had been lonely and hellish for him, but he could get through it, he thought, much better than he could live with a broken heart.

THE APPOINTMENT WITH Dr. Olstead was at eleven in the morning. The two of them left the house early enough to make the drive without having to hurry.

It was the first time Nevada had been back to town in more than a week and she looked around the place with renewed interest.

"It's funny how a little time away from a place makes it all seem new again."

"Guess you've missed it," he said.

Nevada shook her head as she wheeled

the car into the parking lot near a block of medical buildings.

"Actually, I'm surprised how little I have missed it. There's been a few times I got to craving the noise of a television. But other than that, I've enjoyed your parents' house."

His parents' house. Funny that Linc had never thought of the place in that way. To him it was his father's house. Darla hadn't seemed a part of it. Not when she'd hated the place so much.

"Well, give me the bunkhouse any day," he said.

Nevada tried not to feel hurt as she looked over at him. "I guess you miss all your buddies." She smiled wryly. "Men get tired of hearing a woman's chatter and I can't talk horse talk with you. I hope Dr. Olstead will give you some good news and you'll be able to go back to work soon."

She picked up her handbag from the console between them and dropped the key inside. Next to her, Linc unbuckled his seat belt then at the last minute before she opened the door, he reached for her hand.

Nevada turned her face around to his. "Yes?"

He grimaced before he cut his eyes away from her. Even so, Nevada could see something was troubling him. His jaw was tight, his lips pressed to a thin line. She hated seeing him like this. Especially when he'd shown her a glimpse of the gentle man he used to be.

"Uh—a minute ago. That bit I said about the bunkhouse. Don't take that personally. You've done a good job helping me—it's just that I'm more comfortable there with the men."

For some reason his haltingly spoken words saddened her more than anything she could remember and she wound her fingers around his and gently squeezed. "I understand, Linc. Don't try to explain. It'll all be over soon anyway. And I'll be glad for you."

But as for herself, she couldn't imagine what it was going to feel like to go back to her apartment, to live all by herself. There wouldn't be any more breakfasts together. No more sitting on the patio watching the sunrise together. No more helping him into his clothes or sitting close beside him as she tended his bandages. Soon her time with Linc would all be over and she could go back to her happy life and forget about the man with longing written in his eyes and sadness in his voice.

Glancing at her watch, she said, "We'd better go inside. It's almost time for your appointment."

The clinic was full of waiting patients, especially pregnant women and little children. Nevada looked at them and wondered if she would ever be sure enough about someone to start a family with him. As for Linc, he grabbed up a magazine and ignored the whole lot. Including Nevada.

It wasn't long before the nurse stepped out to call Linc's name and usher him back to Dr. Olstead's examining room. Nevada went along with him. Not because he'd asked her to, but because she was his nurse and it would help her care for him better if she heard everything the doctor had to say. She tried to ignore the fact that she wanted to be with him. Just like a wife accompanying her injured or sick husband, she thought with chagrin.

And when Dr. Olstead's nurse began to remove Linc's bandages, Nevada had to fight the urge to push the other woman out of the way and take hold of him herself.

But of course, she had no right or reason to do that so she sat in a plastic chair shoved in one corner of the tiny room while the nurse and the doctor made a thorough examination of Linc's arms and hands.

Thirty minutes later they were back outside the building and as they walked to Nevada's car, one of Linc's rare smiles began to appear on his face.

"Thank God that's over," he said with relief.

"You got a good report."

"Thanks to you," he said.

She scoffed at the compliment. "Anybody can smear medication on a burn. It was nothing."

She walked on ahead of him to the car and for a moment Linc stared thoughtfully after her. He didn't know what had caused the change in her, but something had made her distant, almost indifferent with him. He realized he didn't like it. He wanted her warmth and her smile back. But then he reminded himself that he didn't really deserve Nevada's kindness. Not when he'd been going hot one minute and cold the next; behaving like a jackass who didn't know his head from his tail.

"Is something wrong, Nevada?" he asked as he climbed into the seat next to hers.

Tossing him a glance, she turned the key in the ignition and the engine sprang to life. "Nothing is wrong. Why?"

He shrugged. "I don't know. You just seem a little distant."

Her hand paused on the gearshift. "So? I can't imagine that bothering you."

She put the car into Reverse and gunned it backwards.

"Dr. Olstead said I could go down to the ranch yard and look at the horses," he said.

"If you keep your distance," she reminded him.

"Yeah. Well, it doesn't look like I'm going to make it there anyway. Maybe Skinny will see that all the mares foal as they should and the weanlings are separated from their mothers."

Nevada kept her eyes on the town traffic. "Why aren't you going to make it? Dr. Olstead just gave you a glowing report, not a death sentence."

"I know. But for some reason you're trying to kill me." He scowled at her. "What's the matter with you, anyway?"

Nevada glanced over at him. What *was* the matter, she asked herself. Was it because she could see her time with him soon ending? That even though he'd only kissed her once since they'd been together, that one kiss had shattered all her preconceived notions about men?

"Nothing, I told you. I'm fine. I guess being in the clinic just made me miss working," she lied.

With Dr. Martinez, he thought, as he stared glumly out the windshield. "Guess you'll be happy to get back to working with Victoria. I'm sure she's a good boss."

"The best."

If you want to know anything personal about Nevada, you should ask her yourself.

As Victoria's words rolled through Linc's mind, he glanced thoughtfully over at Nevada.

"Would you like to go to the Wagon Wheel for lunch?"

She stomped on the brake as the car ahead of them suddenly stopped for a left-hand turn. As they bounced to a halt, Nevada looked over at him.

"You're asking me to go out to lunch with you?"

He surprised her with a low chuckle. "Yes. What's the deal? We eat lunch together everyday anyway."

"True. But this time we'll be in public and you'll be buying." And she couldn't imagine why he might want to linger in town with her. But she wasn't going to question his motives. The man needed an outing in the worst kind of way.

A faint smile touched his rugged face. "I can handle it if you can," he said.

At the next intersection Nevada flipped on the blinker and turned down the street that would take them straight to the diner.

"I think I can survive having lunch with

you," she murmured. It was the coming days without him that Nevada was worried about.

Chapter Ten

The Wagon Wheel Café was an eating place that had been in town since the early fifties. Except for a new tile floor and a fresh coat of paint once in a while, it had remained the same simple diner down through the years. The food was good and the eclectic atmosphere was created by the mix of business people dressed in suits and local ranchers in hats and spurs.

Nevada and Linc found a booth in the back of the room and ordered the blue plate special of meat loaf, mashed potatoes, corn and hot rolls. They'd hardly begun to eat when an older man approached their table and greeted Linc.

He turned out to be only one of many to come by their booth and strike up a conversation with Linc. For the most part, Nevada sat quietly eating while Linc answered concerned questions about his health.

She was totally surprised that he seemed to be acquainted with every person in the diner and she said as much to him as they walked out of the building and down the sidewalk to where she'd parked the car.

"You've surprised me, Linc. Here all along I thought you were a stay-at-home kind of guy. Instead, I learn you know half the townspeople."

He shook his head. "I *am* a stay-at-home guy. Each one of those people that came by the table, I met on the ranch," he explained. "You see, anyone who wants to buy a horse from the T Bar K has to go through me. And down through the years we've sold many."

Pausing on the sidewalk she looked at him with interest. "I didn't know you were a trader, too! I've often heard you should never trust a horse trader," she added impishly. "Is that true?"

Chuckling, he took her by the arm and

urged her on down the sidewalk. "Depends on what you're trusting him to do."

THE MEAL AT the diner and meeting up with old friends appeared to have had a positive effect on Linc. Throughout their drive back to the ranch, he was more talkative and the stilted awkwardness that had been building between them since their time in the cave seemed to ease.

Nevada was relieved with the change between them. It was hard enough for her to hide her burgeoning feelings without having to carefully tiptoe around the man, too.

When they finally reached the main ranch yard, Nevada didn't bother asking him if he wanted to park and take a look at the horses. She simply pulled the car over to an out-of-the-way spot next to a pole corral and killed the motor.

"What are you doing?" he asked with surprise.

"Dr. Olstead said you could look at the horses if you didn't touch anything or get too close. I thought you might like to show me some of your favorites."

Surprise flickered in his eyes and then his whole expression softened. "Only if you're interested. You don't have to give me therapy, you know."

"Maybe I'm the one who needs therapy," she teased, then gently touched his arm. "I'm interested, Linc. Otherwise, I wouldn't have stopped."

Grinning faintly, he tugged his hat down on his forehead and reached for the door handle "Okay. Let's go."

The men who were working around the ranch yard for the afternoon were all surprised to see Linc. As they rushed to greet him, Nevada was careful to remind each of them that because their hands were dirty they couldn't touch their boss and risk giving him an infection.

None of the men seemed to care about that, and they all talked to him at length until Linc finally had to send them on their way.

"You didn't have to do that for my sake,"

Nevada told him a few minutes later as they walked toward a fenced corral where several mares were chomping at a hay manger filled with dark-green alfalfa. "There's no hurry."

He shrugged. "Don't worry about the men. They all needed to get back to work anyway."

Once they reached the corral, Linc pointed to the mares. There were two blacks, three sorrels and three grays. All of them were in an advanced state of pregnancy.

"These are just a few of our broodmares that will be foaling soon. About a month before time we put them up in this pen so that we can keep a watch on them."

"They're all so beautiful," Nevada said softly as she gazed at the graceful creatures with their long manes and tails. "Is it common for a mare giving birth to have trouble?"

"Not usually. Most have routine births. But sometimes things go wrong. And when they do, you only have a few minutes to try to correct it. Most mares carry their babies for eleven months, so it's a long wait to get one here. And then sometimes they're still-born. When that happens—well, it really hurts," he murmured.

The emotion in his voice caused her to glance over at him and in that moment as she watched him gazing out at the mares, she realized his rugged body and gruff de-meanor was hiding a huge, soft heart. If he were to ever love a woman he would do so with everything inside him, she decided. There wouldn't be any halves with Linc Ketchum.

But Nevada didn't want to think about him loving a woman. Not unless that woman was her. And since that could never happen, she tried not to think about it at all and focus on the horses.

With his arm curled loosely against her back, Linc guided her to the end of a long barn where a railed fence held at least twenty geldings. Three of them were sad-dled and tethered to a wooden hitching post and Linc explained that the cowboys who'd been riding them had probably come into the bunkhouse for lunch and were planning to go back out on the range again after they ate.

"The rest of this small herd is a portion of our remuda. These are the geldings that the cowboys use every day. They're worked hard, so they require a lot of care. Plenty of feed and hay, morning and night, liniment rubdowns and doctoring. But they're all bred strong. You won't find any fine-boned, timid horses on the T Bar K," he said proudly.

Nevada pointed to a white horse that was splattered with tiny chocolate-brown spots all over his body. "He's gorgeous. If you ever do take me for a ride, Linc, I want to ride him," she told him.

Smiling at her choice, he said, "That's Spotted Bird. He can be a handful at times. But if you pet him and give him a few treats he'll settle right down."

"Sort of like you?" she joked, her brown eyes sparkling.

He chuckled. "Yeah. Sort of like me," he

admitted, then taking her by the arm he led her around to the front of the barn. "Let's go in. I want you to see Miss Lori."

She cast him a concerned look. "I'm not sure you should go inside the barn."

Grimacing, he held out his hands and arms. "I know I'm supposed to be careful. But look at this, Nevada. I don't think anything is going to penetrate all these layers of bandages, do you?"

As Nevada studied his injured limbs, she understood that agreeing to let him walk into the barn would be far better medicine than worrying about infection.

"We're going to act like it won't," she said finally. "So let's go. I want to see this Miss Lori that you've been fretting about."

A broad smile slowly parted his lips and, while watching the transformation come over his face, it suddenly dawned on Nevada that making this man happy had become far too important to her.

Two huge doors were opened at the end of the building and Linc guided her inside where they walked down a wide alleyway filled with the pungent scent of pine-wood shavings. On either side of them were rows of stalls most of which appeared to be empty at the moment.

"At least this barn was saved," she said as she looked all around her. Everything was exceptionally clean. She could smell the disinfectant which had been used to wash down walls and clean water troughs. "Where was the barn that burned?"

"I'll show you when we leave. It was about fifty yards from here. Thank God none of the sparks set any of the other buildings around it on fire."

They reached a fence with a latched gate. Linc opened it and ushered her into an area closed off from the rest of the structure. A black mare with a star on her forehead was inside the large lot. In one corner Skinny was sitting in an old wooden chair tilted onto its back legs and resting against the fence. The old man was softly playing a harmonica and he finished the little tune before he lowered the instrument to greet the two of them.

"Well, look who's here." A big grin spread over his wrinkled old face as he got up from the chair to join them at the opening of the foaling area. "I thought you weren't supposed to be around the barn."

Linc jerked his head toward Nevada. "She gave me permission."

Skinny's eyes twinkled with appreciation as he looked at Nevada. "You must be even smarter than you are pretty, Miss Nevada. You gonna let him hang around a while?"

Nevada regretfully shook her head. "I'm sorry, Skinny. I can't let him stay but a few minutes. He wanted to show me Miss Lori."

The old wrangler pointed a finger at the black mare. "Well, there she is. She's a beauty, ain't she?"

"Gorgeous," Nevada agreed. "Is it okay if I pet her?"

"Of course," Linc assured her. "Just walk up to her slowly, with your shoulder to her and don't look her straight in the eye until she smells you."

Nevada left the two men and walked over to where the mare was munching on a hay bag filled with alfalfa. Slowly, so as not to startle her, she did as Linc had instructed. After a few moments she was able to reach out and touch the mare's neck with soft, gentle strokes.

Miss Lori turned her head and gazed at Nevada with trusting brown eyes. The exchange with the animal touched her in a way she would never have expected, and she suddenly understood the deep connection Linc felt to his horses. They were truly his family and he felt safe with them because they loved him unconditionally. They would never purposely hurt him.

"She likes you."

Linc's words were murmured gently next to Nevada's ear and she realized she'd been so involved with the mare, she hadn't heard him walk up behind her.

"I'm glad. What would she do if I stroked her on the face? Do horses like that?"

Her question caused his lips to tilt with

amusement. "Of course they like it. Don't you?"

She wrinkled her nose at him. "Depends on who's doing the stroking."

A sensual glint sparked his eyes as he reached for her hand and placed it on the mare's nose.

"Picky about that, are you?"

Nevada sucked in an edgy breath as the front of his body brushed against the back of hers. "Much pickier than you think," she muttered.

He didn't say anything to that, and she glanced over her shoulder to see that his expression had sobered. After his playful warmth of this afternoon the sight chilled her.

"I need to talk to Skinny about a few things," he said. "I'll be ready to go in just a minute or two."

Nodding, she turned her gaze back to the mare and told herself to quit acting like a foolish teenage girl. It was crazy for her to allow her feelings to get all tangled up with Linc Ketchum's moods. From the way

Dr. Olstead had talked this afternoon, Linc would probably be free of his bandages in another week. After that he would allow him to do light work. At least, he could use his hands enough to see to his own needs. That meant Nevada's job would be finished. And the best thing she could do right now was get ready for the exit.

On the short drive up the mountain to the house, Linc was quiet and Nevada didn't try to engage him in small talk. She wasn't exactly in a talking mood herself. She was feeling a bit defeated and even more angry with herself.

For the past ten of her twenty-five years, she'd pretty much taken care of herself. She had not relied on anyone for financial or emotional support. She had gritted through the poverty and loneliness, and the insecurities of being without a dependable family. She'd finally carved out a niche for herself. She had a good job that she loved. And though she was far from rich, she was secure. She didn't need a man mixed permanently into her life. Not Linc. Not any man.

LATER THAT NIGHT, long after they'd eaten dinner and she'd cleared away the dishes, the telephone rang.

Answering it, she found Victoria's husband, Jess, the under-sheriff of San Juan County, on the other end.

"Has Linc already gone to bed?" he asked.

"I don't think so. Let me go find him," she said and put down the phone to hurry through the house.

She found him on the front porch, reading a book beneath the dim glow of a coal-oil lamp. Early in the week, she'd caught him doing the same thing and had asked him why he didn't go inside to read by the light of a proper lamp. He'd told her he felt best when he was outside and that the pioneers who'd settled the nation before them had read just fine by coal-oil lamps.

Nevada hadn't argued with him then and she didn't stop to now as he put down his book and looked up at her.

"You have a telephone call. It's Jess."

Rising from his chair, he blew out

the lamp and headed toward the door. "Thanks," he called over his shoulder.

Nevada followed him back into the house but rather than return to the kitchen and intrude on his phone call, she went to her room and began to prepare for bed. She brushed her teeth and cleaned her face and was sitting on the dressing bench brushing her hair when she heard a knock at her door. Turning around, she saw Linc standing in the open doorway. A stricken look was on his face and her heart plummeted.

"What's wrong? What's happened?" she questioned.

He stepped into the room and took a seat on the foot of her bed, something he'd never done before. He was obviously disturbed.

"Jess called to tell me that he'd just gotten out of a meeting with Sheriff Perez and the fire marshal." His dark gaze caught hers. "The fire at the barn has been ruled to have been arson."

Stunned at the idea that anyone could do such a horrific thing, Nevada could only stare at him. "Arson? I can't believe it. Are they certain?"

He nodded and there was a sick, almost fatalistic look on his face. "Yes. They're sure. The fire marshal says there were two ignition sites, one at each end of the building, and some sort of chemical was used as an accelerator."

"I just can't believe it," Nevada said again in a dazed voice. "Who would do such a thing? You could have been killed! You nearly were!"

Ignoring the implications to his own safety, he said in stunned disbelief, "The horses. How could anyone deliberately set out to kill a barn full of innocent animals? I—"

He stopped and shook his head in dismay. Nevada could see he was clearly shaken by the news Jess had given him.

Feeling the strong urge to console him, Nevada left the dressing table and took a seat next to him on the edge of the mattress.

"I'm so sorry, Linc. So terribly sorry.

Your family has already been through so much with the Rider murder and then Jess nearly being fatally shot. I can't believe that someone else is out to hurt you Ketchums."

"More like out to hurt me. It wasn't unusual for me to stay all night in that barn. Before it was destroyed, that's where I kept most of the pregnant mares and our prize stallion. It was just by the grace of God that there weren't any newborn colts in the barn that night." With a weary groan he lifted one hand and raked it over his face. "Jess is sending out deputies to guard the other buildings in the ranch yard until Ross can come up with some security guards of his own. Hell, what is that going to say to all the people who come here to buy cattle and horses? They'll all be too scared to set a foot on the place!"

Nevada had never seen a raging fire up close, but she could easily imagine the horror of one. The idea that someone had purposely set out to hurt or kill Linc made her shudder.

Reaching over, she placed her hand on

his knee. "Linc, try not to think about it," she urged. "Just let Sheriff Perez take care of things. He'll find the person behind all this."

He sucked in a long, shaky breath and then released it in one weary whoosh. "I hope he does. Because if I find him first, I'm going to put these hands around his neck and choke the hell right out of him."

The threat in his voice was cool and deliberate and Nevada had no doubt that he meant what he said.

Suddenly she was very scared for his safety and she clutched his upper arm with both hands.

"Linc, please, don't do anything foolish. You've already been seriously hurt. I—I don't want anything else to happen to you."

Slowly, the dark revenge in his eyes began to fade away and he looked at her with a bit of wonder.

"If I didn't know better," he said softly, "I'd think you really meant that."

Without any warning, Nevada's heart started swelling with emotions and her brown eyes grew misty as she looked up at him. "I do mean it, Linc. I mean it very much."

The room had been quiet before, but now there didn't seem to be any sound at all as the seconds slid by and his gaze slowly searched her face. Finally his attention focused on her lips and caused heat to surge through her body with lightning speed. Desire boiled up inside her and she couldn't stop herself from leaning into him and tilting her face up to his.

"Nevada. Nevada."

Her name was all he said before he bent his head and placed his lips over hers.

He kissed her sweetly, gently, then pulled back to look at her once more.

Nevada could feel the naked longing on her face and knew that he could see it, too, but her desire for him had grown far too strong to hide.

"Make love to me, Linc."

His bandaged hands rested gently on her shoulders. "You don't know what you're saying."

Her gaze didn't waver on his. "I know exactly what I'm saying."

In the back of Linc's mind, he understood that to reach for Nevada would be as dangerous as reaching for a stick of dynamite. But these past days he'd spent being near her and desperately wanting her had taken a toll on him. He was weak from the constant exertion of trying to resist her.

And why should he keep fighting? he asked himself. The two of them were consenting adults. What happened between them tonight would have no bearing on tomorrow. And maybe, just maybe, having her in his bed would put an end to this maddening ache in his loins.

Without another thought, he pulled her toward him and she fell willingly into his arms.

Over and over Linc kissed her until her arms wound tightly around his neck and she tugged them both down on the mattress.

Lying face to face, he pulled his head back far enough so that his gaze could delve into hers. "I've wanted you from the moment I saw you. But are you sure you want me?" he asked.

With a sensual groan, she lifted a hand to his face and gently stroked his cheek. "I want you, Linc. More than anything," she told him as the truth of those words shattered the resistance she'd desperately been trying to hold on to.

"Little one. My sweet," he murmured.

His soft words of affection caused joy to pour into her heart and she closed her eyes in blissful anticipation as he brought his lips over hers once again.

His searching mouth quickly sent her senses scattering in all directions and before she realized what she was doing, her fingers were loosening the buttons on his shirt, her palms were spreading flat against his hair-roughened chest.

Groaning with pleasure, he deserted her lips to press a moist, tingly trail down the side of her throat.

"Damn it," he murmured with agony. "I can't undress you. My hands can't feel your skin. And I want to feel you, Nevada. So badly."

His urgent words were like an instant aphrodisiac and all she wanted was to please him, to give him anything and everything he wanted. She'd never felt anything close to this before and the reality of what was happening made her whole body hum with love.

And it was love, she told herself. She didn't just want Linc's body. She wanted his heart, his soul to bind with hers. She wanted the two of them to be together like this forever.

"I'll be your hands. Just lean back and let me undress you," she whispered fervently. "Let me make love to you."

He did as she asked, and as Nevada began to remove his boots and then his clothing, she noticed he was watching her through green eyes that were simmering with a fire of their own.

With her gaze fastened firmly on his face, she finally removed his jeans. He was wearing boxer shorts beneath the jeans and she deliberately left them where they were. Even so, she could tell he was already firmly aroused and the sight of his desire left her whole body glowing with heat and her cheeks blooming with color.

"Are you blushing?" he asked teasingly as he watched her fumble with the buttons on her own blouse.

Nevada quickly turned her back to him. "No. It's the dim light in here. In fact, I think we should turn off the lamp."

She started to skirt the bed so that she could reach the small lamp sitting on a table near the headboard. But before she could take more than two steps, Linc caught her by the arm.

"Forget the lamp," he murmured huskily. "I want to see you. I've been wanting to see you for days now."

Nevada had never been naked in front of any man before, and normally the mere thought of being in such a vulnerable position was enough to embarrass her. But Linc's eager request made her feel beautiful and wanted and she wanted to give back to him.

The blue shirt she'd been wearing finally hit the floor and soon her jeans followed. Beneath she was wearing a pale yellow panty and bra set that was made of lace and satin triangles that did little more than cover her nipples and the patch of black hair growing at the apex of her thighs. The soft color glowed like liquid gold against her brown skin and Linc groaned with pleasure as she lay down next to him.

"The rest should be easy enough for you to get off," she whispered against his cheek.

With a low chuckle, he gently rolled her onto her back. "I might just have to chew these things off."

For the next few minutes that was exactly what Nevada thought he was going to do as his mouth explored every crevice, every hill and valley of her body.

Finally, he raised his head and muttered thickly, "Oh honey. Honey. I've got to make you mine. All mine."

Awkwardly, his bandaged fingers pulled

at her lingerie, and though she could have helped him remove the pieces of clothing, she understood he needed to do this much of the chore himself.

Once the satin and lace were finally out of the way, he started to position himself over her, but Nevada quickly put a hand against his chest and guided him back to the mattress.

"You can't put pressure on your hands," she gently reminded him. "You'll damage all the healing."

"But—"

He didn't finish the question. He didn't have to as Nevada straddled his waist and flipped her long black hair over her shoulders.

"You little siren," he murmured thickly. "I should have known."

His hands came up to cup her small breasts and though his bandages came between their skins, his touch still excited her beyond anything she could have imagined.

With a groan deep in her throat, she lowered one shoulder so that his mouth could reach her breast. The simple invitation was enough to tell him what she needed and he gladly complied by gently biting down on the chocolate-brown nipple.

"Oooh. Oh Linc. I didn't—know it would be—like this."

Easing back from her slightly, he could see her head was thrown back, her eyes squeezed tightly shut. She was as taut as a violin string just waiting to be plucked and stroked.

"Sure you did, baby. Come here," he crooned. "Come here and let me love you."

With a little help, he pushed his boxer shorts down over his feet and then, placing his hands on both sides of her shapely hips, he guided her up and over his rigid manhood.

The intimate folds of her body were hot and moist and the pleasure of entering her turned Linc's blood to liquid fire. Every nerve, every particle of his body screamed at him to hurry, hurry. But he'd never believed this moment would happen and he wanted it to last. He wanted to watch her face as he slowly filled her body.

Sweat gathered on his face and she began to say his name over and over in a thick, choked voice like a pleading mantra begging him to end her agony.

Finally with a downward tug on her hips, Linc gave one final thrust and her delicious body closed around him like a tight, loving hand.

Nevada bit down hard on her bottom lip, but she couldn't prevent the loud sob from escaping into the quiet bedroom. Yet it wasn't the sound that suddenly paralyzed Linc. It was the thin barrier he'd encountered at the very last moment as he'd joined their bodies.

She was a virgin! A virgin!

"Nevada! What—why didn't you tell me?" he groaned.

He started to push her off him, but she wouldn't budge. Instead, she leaned down and cupped her hands against the sides of his face. "Because it doesn't matter."

Chapter Eleven

"Like hell, I—"

"This is what I want," she interrupted. "And you don't want to stop now, do you?"

He should stop, Linc thought. He should slide away from her this very minute, leave the bedroom and never look back. But his body absolutely refused to listen to any part of that suggestion. Especially when her hips began a slow thrust that turned him inside out.

"You know I don't," he muttered gruffly and then with a groan of surrender, he began to match his movements to hers.

In all of his adult life Linc had never felt such intense pleasure, and though he realized he needed to go slowly to initiate her to their intimate coupling, he couldn't hold back his hunger. Nor could he hide it from her.

Tugging her head down, he feasted on her lips as his hands cupped her rounded bottom and urged her to an even faster pace.

Her breathing became rapid and so did his. Her long hair swung forward and cocooned them inside a curtain of black satin.

Eventually, Nevada's arms got tired and she fell over Linc with an exhausted thump.

"I'm sorry, Linc. My arms—" she said between pants for air.

"Sssh," he whispered as he rolled her onto her back. "Let me finish this."

"Your hands—"

"My hands are the last thing you need to be thinking about," he told her. Then, straddling her body, he lowered himself over her and rested his weight on his elbows. "See how good this is."

Nevada wanted to answer, but she couldn't. His movements were taking her breath away, sending her to a place she'd never been before.

Bright, beautiful stars began to parade behind the back of her closed eyes. Suddenly she felt herself floating upward toward the stars in that velvety sky, until something deep inside her exploded like a meteor shower.

At the same time the thrust of Linc's hips grew frenzied, and with a great groan, he clutched her desperately to him and spilled the warm seeds of his manhood.

It was some time before Nevada was capable of speaking a word. By then Linc had rolled his weight to her side and was studying her with dark, drowsy eyes.

Turning onto her side, she leaned forward and pressed a kiss upon his lips. She had never tasted anything so good in her life, and she wanted to keep on kissing him, but she could see that he wanted to say something so she pulled back and waited.

"Why were you a virgin, Nevada?"

His question seemed ludicrous and she chuckled softly. "I was a virgin because I'd never made love to a man. That's the medical explanation."

"Damn it, I don't want some clinical reason! You—"

She placed a forefinger over his lips. "It's not all that perplexing, Linc. I'd just never met a man I wanted to make love to until you."

He outwardly winced, and she wondered what the reaction meant. Was he already regretting making love to her?

"But you—you let me believe—you talked about your boyfriends and—"

"And you jumped to conclusions. Like a lot of people do where I'm concerned. Just because I have friends that happen to be male, everyone believes I'm a sex siren or something." She rolled her eyes with amusement. "Nothing could be further from the truth."

"Why?"

Her brows lifted in question and he repeated, "Why? Didn't you *feel* anything physical for them?"

She sighed. "Linc, I don't go around experimenting with men. In fact—" Biting down on her lip, she glanced away from him.

"What?" he urged.

"I've been careful to keep my relationships with men only as friendships. That's the way I've always wanted it. And that's the way I always intended it to be. But, you've come along and changed all that."

He couldn't believe any of this. All along, he'd thought Nevada was experienced with men. He'd believed she'd considered them as nothing more than entertainment. At least, that's what he'd wanted to believe. Part of him had desperately been trying to ignore the kind, caring woman who more often than not had put his needs before her own. And now he had to face the fact she'd offered him her innocence and he'd taken it so carelessly.

Linc moved closer, lifted his hand to her brow and gently pushed back her tumbled hair. "You should have told me beforehand, Nevada. I would have—"

"What?" she interrupted. "Not made

love to me? Left the room like I had small-pox?"

"I don't know," he admitted truthfully. "But at least I could have been more gentle with you."

Groaning, she scooted forward until the front of her body was pressing into his and her arm was curved around his waist.

"You *were* gentle, Linc. You were perfect. Perfect," she repeated in a whisper as she rubbed her cheek against his chest.

The adoration he heard in her voice pricked him with fear. She wasn't supposed to be all warm and fuzzy and loving toward him. And his heart shouldn't be swelling with the sort of emotions that made him want to hold her close and never let go.

"Honey. You'll know different. When you find a good man."

She pulled her head back and peered dreamily up at him. "I have found a good man."

Linc's heart jerked with a feeling that was both sweet and frightening. "You don't know what you're saying," he said in a husky whisper. "You don't know me, not really."

She smiled at him. A wide show of affection that was full of sensual invitation. "Then maybe you'd better let me learn more."

It was time to stop this thing that was happening between them, Linc told himself. If he didn't stop it both of them were going to suffer. But even the thought of the misery to come was not strong enough to make him move out of her arms.

"Maybe I'd better," he said and with a murmur of pleasure he brought his lips down on hers.

When Nevada woke the next morning, the space next to her was empty and the morning sun was already slanting weakly through the nearby window. She could smell coffee and sausage and the distinct scent of warm flour tortillas filtering through the house, telling her that Linc had been busy in the kitchen.

Linc. She said his name over and over in her mind as she stretched her stiff muscles and climbed out of bed. He was the man she'd thought she would never meet. And though it scared her to think of committing her life to another person, she realized she didn't want to step into the future without him. He made her feel special and loved and she desperately wanted to make him feel the same way.

After tossing on her robe and splashing her face with warm water, she hurried out to the kitchen. She found Linc sitting at the table, his bandaged hands curled around a mug of coffee.

He looked up as she entered the room and smiling she went to him and placed a kiss upon his forehead.

"Good morning," she greeted.

"Good morning."

"I smell food. Have you eaten breakfast yet?" she asked.

Careful to avoid her gaze, he shook his head. "No. I've been waiting on you."

"Linc," she scolded sweetly. "You didn't have to do that. Besides, you should have woken me. I've slept way too late. I hope you haven't needed me for anything."

Oh, he needed her all right, but not as a nurse, Linc thought. But he kept that fact to himself. He could never let her learn exactly what making love to her had done to him. It would give her power over him. And he couldn't allow that. He could never repeat the mistakes of his father.

"I've been fine," he said dully, then ignoring her hand on his shoulder, he rose to his feet. "I've made breakfast tacos. I'll get them."

Nevada trailed after him and painful regret sliced through him as she stared up at him in confusion.

"Linc? Is something wrong?"

"No. Nothing is wrong," he said. "I'm just hungry. Aren't you?"

Her brow remained puckered as she studied his face. "Yes, I am. But—"

She stopped as he turned to pour coffee into a waiting mug. "Here." He handed her the cup. "Get your cream and I'll take the tacos over to the table."

"Linc, aren't you even going to kiss me good morning?" Surely she deserved that much of a greeting from him, she thought.

He looked away from her. "Don't you think you had enough kissing last night?" he asked sharply.

Stunned by the total change in him, she quietly walked over to the breakfast table and sank onto the end of the bench.

Behind her, Linc gathered up two plates and a basket full of tacos and carried them over to the center of the table. Nevada didn't say anything as he shoved one of the plates and the basket in her direction. She simply picked up one of the tacos and began to eat.

After several minutes of silence had passed, he said in a distant voice, "Look, Nevada, if you got up this morning thinking we were going to start playing house together, then I'm sorry, you got it all wrong."

Funny that he should choose those words, Nevada thought sadly. As a young girl she'd never had the chance to *play* house. She'd had to behave as a grown woman and take care of things that her mother hadn't been capable of dealing with. There had been many times she'd cleaned up after her drunken father and helped him to bed. And back then, she'd vowed to herself that she would never let another man disappoint or hurt her in any way. Too bad she hadn't been able to stick to that vow, she thought.

"I didn't think we'd *play* anything," Nevada said soberly. "And I didn't think I'd wake up this morning to be insulted by you."

A shamed expression suddenly washed over his dark face and he placed his taco on the table, then moved down the bench so that he was sitting only inches from her.

Nevada quivered with hurt and longing as he lifted his hand and touched her cheek.

"I'm sorry, Nevada. I should never have said that. I don't know why I did."

Tears suddenly misted her eyes and she looked down at her lap rather than have him see them. "It's all right, Linc. I understand."

"I doubt it," he said grimly.

Her head jerked up and their gazes locked. "Why do you say that? You think I don't understand that all of this is just as new for you as it is for me?"

He let out a heavy sigh. "Look, Nevada. What happened between us last night was very, very nice. But—"

"But you didn't really mean anything serious by it," she finished for him.

Her voice was thin and flat and the mist in her eyes was growing thicker, but she no longer cared if he knew how much she was beginning to hurt.

He shook his head. "I think you were aware of that from the very beginning."

Yes, maybe she had been, Nevada thought. Maybe in the back of her mind she'd always known that Linc was a free spirit, a loner at heart. Sex with a woman was just that for him and nothing else. Yet the moment he'd kissed her, she'd believed there was something special, something magical flowing from him to her. Apparently she'd been a fool to think he'd felt anything but physical pleasure.

"Linc, it wasn't like I sat for hours and contemplated what was about to happen," she tried to explain. "But even if I had, I wouldn't have changed anything. I would still have wanted you to make love to me."

With a groan of frustration he looked away from her and raked a hand over his dark, tumbled hair. He looked tired, she thought. But more than that he looked anguished, and the idea that she was putting him through such torment was enough to crack her heart right down the middle.

"Nevada, I don't how to explain. Maybe all I should say is that—last night can't happen again. It *won't* happen again. Understand?"

Stiffly, her head jerked back and forth. "No. I don't understand. Why? I thought last night was a beginning for us."

He swallowed hard and then before she could guess his intentions, he rose from the table and crossed over to the kitchen sink where he stood with his back to her and stared out the window.

"There can't be an *us,* Nevada. That's what I'm trying to get across to you."

Nevada left her seat and when she reached his side, she carefully lifted his bandaged hand and cradled it to her face.

"I don't think you really mean that, Linc."

He swallowed hard as he tried to rid himself of the ball of pain burning his throat and creeping into his chest. "I have to mean it," he said flatly. "I've been a bachelor for many years now. That isn't going to change. For you or anyone."

"Why?"

He pulled his hand away from her grasp. "You shouldn't have to ask. You've already told me that you didn't want to get serious about a man. Obviously you have reasons of your own for staying single and I have mine."

She nodded glumly. "That's true. I never wanted this to happen to me. I actually prayed that it wouldn't. Because I know firsthand what it does to a woman to depend solely and completely on a man. My mother adored my father. For a long time she refused to see his shortcomings. And then when his boozing and womanizing became too much to ignore, she still loved him so much she couldn't let him go. It was a horrible situation. Now she drinks to forget it all." Shaking her head, she searched his face. "That's why this scares me, because I've fallen in love with you."

Linc was stunned by her revelation and even though he was telling himself he didn't want or need her love, joy was pouring into his heart. "Nevada, last night wasn't love—"

"Don't, Linc! Just don't ruin everything for me. As far as I'm concerned it was love. And don't try to tell me that all I'm feeling is physical infatuation. I began caring for you the very first day I arrived. I tried to stop my feelings then. But I couldn't. And now I find I don't want to."

He was quaking inside and for once he was glad his hands were hidden behind all the bandages. They were shaking like those of a man who'd drunk too much and slept too little.

"I'm sorry about that, Nevada. If you think I set out to hurt you, you're wrong. Last night just happened and now for both our sakes we've got to put it behind us."

"Why?" she demanded. "I thought what happened between us was wonderful. Wasn't it that way for you?"

He felt sick as he turned away from her and walked over to the windows to stare unseeingly at the distant San Juan Mountains. He couldn't tell her the truth, Linc thought. He couldn't let her know that making love to her had turned him inside out and his world upside down. Linc had always believed sex was just sex, a pleasurable act between a man and a woman. But last night in Nevada's arms he'd experienced something far greater than pleasure. He'd felt linked to her in a deeply spiritual way and that idea was still making him shake with fear.

"Yes, Nevada. It was special," he said in

a low, hoarse voice. "But that part of things doesn't matter."

Marching over to him, she forced him to turn and face her. "Doesn't matter?" she asked angrily. "Does *anything* matter to you? Is there anyone on this earth that you care about, other than yourself?"

His expression closed off like a curtain falling over the last scene of a tragic play. "That's a hell of a thing to say."

"That's nothing to what I'd like to say to you," she said tightly.

"What's wrong with you, anyway, Nevada? I understand you were a virgin, but surely you weren't naive enough to think sex equaled a proposal of marriage."

Nevada actually had to clench her fingers to keep from raising her hand and slapping him. "The only thing I was naive about was thinking you had a heart!"

"You've taken my blood pressure enough, you ought to know!" he spat back at her.

The anger and pain boiling up in her head made her lash back at him. "Well you can bet your last dollar that I won't be guilty of checking your blood pressure again. It's obvious you have ice water in your veins!"

He started to make a retort, but Nevada wasn't about to hang around to hear it. She'd already heard far more than she could stand.

"Save it, Linc, I don't want to hear anything else you have to say," she muttered and then hurried out of the kitchen.

By the time she reached the bedroom, her legs were so weak and shaky she could hardly make it to the bed. She sank onto the edge of the mattress and dropped her face into her hands.

This morning when she'd first wakened, she'd felt such a burst of sweet happiness. Making love to Linc had made her whole world bright and beautiful. Too bad her joy couldn't have lasted past breakfast, she thought bitterly.

She was biting back tears, trying to tell herself that he wasn't worth one drop of the salty water running down her cheeks, when she heard him knock on the door.

Deliberately ignoring him, she stared at the wall and desperately tried to swallow away the fiery pain in her throat.

"Nevada. May I come in?"

She didn't answer. She couldn't. It was all she could do to keep the sobs in her chest from bursting past her lips.

Silent moments passed and then she felt his hand upon her back, his fingers threading gently through her tangled hair.

"Nevada, I'm sorry. I'm a bastard. That's all I can say."

Still incapable of looking at him, Nevada shook her head. "No, you could say more if you just would. If it's me—if you've decided you—just don't like me, then tell me. That's all I ask. Tell me the real reason you're trying so hard to push me away."

His hand continued to stroke her back and she could only think of last night and all the ways he'd touched her. Somewhere among all those kisses and touches and whispers, a certainty had filled her heart.

Linc was supposed to be her other half. He was the man who was meant to love her, give her children, protect her from the harsh realities of the world.

He sighed. And then in a soft, low voice, he said, "All right. You told me about your family, your parents and all the trouble they'd had. Well, it was pretty much the same way for me. My parents treated their marriage as a prison sentence more than anything else. After what I saw them go through I knew I didn't want any part of it. And I sure didn't want to put a child of mine through it."

Twisting her head around, she stared at him with a wry sort of hope that stabbed Linc right in the chest.

"That's exactly the way I've always seen things. And that's the main reason I was a virgin. But being here with you, Linc, has changed my way of thinking. I love being close to you, I love living with you. I don't want that to change."

"It has to change," he interrupted flatly.

"Because I'm not capable of taking that sort of chance with you or any woman."

A mixture of pain and anger tightened her features. "Why? Because of your mother? Do you think I would be like her?"

Her questions stung him, and he pulled back to stare at her. "What do you know about my mother anyway?"

Nevada could see she was treading on dangerous ground, but she didn't allow that to stop her. Now wasn't the time to tippy-toe around the main issue.

"Only what you've told me," she admitted. "But that's enough to understand that she must have broken your heart when she left here."

"Who told you that?" he muttered.

"Marina. She's been worried about you because she's been having dreams about your mother."

"Bah!" he snorted. "Marina's dreams are just that—dreams. That old housekeeper just likes to gossip and keep things stirred up."

"Linc! The only pot Marina stirs is her

cooking pot. So don't belittle her! She loves you."

Dropping his head, Linc pinched the bridge of his nose. "Yeah. You're right. Hell, she's always been more of a mother to me than my own mother ever was."

"I can't believe your mother didn't love you. Even mine cared about me in her own way. She just had too many problems of her own to be a good mother. Maybe that's the way it was with yours," she reasoned.

Linc lifted his head to look at her and for the first time in his life, he realized he wanted, needed to talk about his mother.

"My mother hated this ranch. She told my father so every day. She wanted him to move to someplace where there was culture and sidewalks, a city where she could buy expensive high heels and get her nails done."

Nevada rolled her eyes. "She could have done that here. If she'd wanted to."

Linc rolled his eyes. "Not in the fashion she wanted. You see, she came from a fairly wealthy family in San Antonio. She was the epitome of a beautiful Texas socialite. Obviously she didn't fit in here and the more my father tried to force her to fit in, the worse things got."

Nevada considered what he was telling her. "She must have known what she was getting into when she married him. This sort of life shouldn't have been that much of a surprise to her," she reasoned. "Maybe your parents had other issues. Things you didn't know about."

Linc's head swung back and forth in disbelief. "Nothing should have made her walk away from here and never look back."

Nevada's eyes widened. "Marina told me that your mother remarried shortly after Randolf's death and that she tried to get you to go back east with her. You didn't want to go?"

"No. I was a teenager by then. This ranch had been my home for all my life. My cousins were like my own siblings. I didn't want to leave my home or family. From the time I was a little boy, I knew I wanted to do what my father and my uncle did. I wanted to be a cowboy, a rancher with lots of horses that everyone would prize and want to own. If I'd gone away with her to some city, I would have dried up and withered away or turned into a rebellious juvenile delinquent."

Nevada tended to agree. Linc was not the sort of man who'd be content to look up at street lamps rather than a sky full of stars.

"I can understand why you stayed," Nevada said softly. "This is where you felt at home. And that's something I've always wanted. Something I've always dreamed about having. A real home with a family that laughed and loved and stuck together through hard times."

Anguish filled his green eyes. "I'm sorry you've never had that, Nevada. I wish I could be the man to give it all to you. But I don't have it in me and it would be disastrous for both of us if I tried."

Instead of arguing that point, Nevada asked, "How long has it been since you've heard from your mother?"

He let out a sound that was somewhere

between a bitter laugh and a snort. "More than twenty years. She was pretty upset that I stayed behind here on the ranch, and for several months I received a few letters and some phone calls from her. But then suddenly they all stopped and that was it. None of us ever heard from Darla Ketchum Carlton again."

"How odd."

"Hell, it was more than odd. It was downright mean," he said, then with a heavy sigh, he got up from his seat beside her and began to walk listlessly around the bedroom. "But then I guess I wasn't a very good son. At least, not to her. I stayed here with Aunt Amelia and Uncle Tucker. They became my parents and she was left out. Maybe I'm the person who's always been wrong here, Nevada. I don't know. That's why—" He paused and looked at her with sad regret. "It's best I always live alone. It's best that I not try to make any woman happy. Especially you."

Chapter Twelve

For the remainder of the day, Nevada couldn't decide what to do. It was apparent that she couldn't sway Linc's way of thinking. At least, she couldn't sway him with talk. Except for when she changed his bandages and choked down the supper Marina brought to them, he avoided her completely. And by that evening, she'd decided that she'd been stupid to believe he cared for her in a special way. Obviously he didn't. And there wasn't any use of her throwing herself at him. She wanted his love, but not that way.

That night when she helped Linc out of his clothes, she kept her touch as impersonal as possible and hurried through the task without ever meeting his gaze. Later, she went to bed feeling like a cold, empty shell and as she lay beneath the light cover all she could think about was Linc lying next to her and how right it had felt to give herself to him.

Nevada tossed and turned for several hours and was finally about to drift off to sleep, when a sound from Linc's room caused her to sit straight up in the bed.

Had he yelled or cried out?

Quickly, she jumped out of bed and ignoring her robe, hurried across the hallway to the open doorway of his bedroom. The faint night lights running along the baseboards in the hallway were enough to allow her to see the outline of his body in bed and fear struck her as she watched him thrash fitfully back and forth upon the mattress.

"Linc." His name whispered from her lips as she hurried to the bedside.

As she leaned over him, she could hear him muttering names and something about stopping the flames.

"Linc, wake up!" She shook his shoulder once, then twice before the thrashing finally stopped and he stared up at her through glazed eyes.

"Nevada? What—are you doing?"

She sat down on the edge of the bed. "You cried out in your sleep. You must have been having a nightmare. Are you okay now?"

He looked around him as though he wasn't quite sure where they were. "Yeah. I think so." He touched his upper arm to his forehead and it came away wet. "I guess I got hot. I'm sweating."

"You were saying something about flames and names that I suppose belong to some of your horses. Junie and Angel."

He nodded, then allowed his head to fall tiredly back against the pillow. "They're two of my best mares. They were the last ones I pulled from the fire. We'd just made it out of the barn when the roof collapsed."

Nevada's heart ached to comfort him and before she could stop herself she reached out and placed her hand on his damp brow. "Try not to think about it now," she mur-

mured gently. "Can I get you something?
Do something for you?"

She could see him closing himself off
from her as he turned his eyes away and
stared at the wall.

"No. Not unless you can cut these damn
bandages off," he said gruffly. "Maybe
then you could get back to your own life
and I can get back to mine."

Nevada's heart was heavy and numb as
she slowly rose from the bedside. "Sorry.
I wish I could. I wish you'd never been
burned and I had never agreed to help a
friend," she said in a stricken voice, then
turned and hurried out of the room.

THE NEXT MORNING when she entered the
kitchen, she discovered Linc had already
eaten breakfast without her and somehow
he'd managed to button his jeans. As for
his shirt, it was the first time she'd ever
seen him in only a T-shirt and he looked almost naked to her, but she didn't make any
comment about it. Nor did she scold him
for putting enough pressure on his fingers

to button his jeans. She knew why he was doing it and she knew right then and there that their days together were over.

After she'd downed a few bites of toast and jelly, she went to her room and called Victoria's office. The moment the other woman heard Nevada's voice, she quickly asked, "What's wrong? Has Linc hurt himself?"

"No. It's nothing like that. I called to see if you were going to be in your office all morning. I'd like to come by and talk to you. It's very important."

"You mean you're going to leave Linc there by himself? You're on the phone with me now, Nevada. Can't we talk like this?"

Even though she was enclosed in her room, she glanced around to make sure Linc wasn't eavesdropping. "I'd rather not. It's too personal."

Victoria let out a long sigh. "Oh dear, this sounds bad."

It *was* bad, Nevada thought, sadly. She'd never felt such anguish in her whole life. "I'll tell you about it when I get there," Nevada told her. "Give me about an hour. If you're in with a patient, I'll wait in your office."

"All right," Victoria agreed, and Nevada quickly said good-bye.

Once she'd hung up the telephone, she quickly packed all her things and left the cases sitting neatly on the bed. She wasn't going to carry them through the house and show Linc her intentions until she'd had a chance to talk with Victoria first. The woman had hired her for this job and she was the person who deserved an explanation.

Minutes later, she told Linc she had to drive into town on business. As she headed her little car down the mountain, she tried not to think that it would be one of the last times she would ever see this wild, beautiful place. Would she ever stop thinking of it as home?

At the clinic she found Victoria engaged with a patient, so she went to the doctor's office to wait. It wasn't long before Victoria hurried into the room. She took hold of Nevada by both shoulders.

"All right. What's happened? You want to quit, don't you? I could hear it in your voice."

Dropping her head, Nevada swung it back and forth. "I'm sorry, Victoria. I realize that doesn't mean much. But there are circumstances that—well, I just can't stay under the same roof with Linc anymore. He doesn't want me there. And I feel very awkward, to say the least."

Her face puckered with confusion, Victoria released her hold on Nevada and crossed the room to the leather chair behind her desk. As she sank into it and crossed her legs, she repeated, "Doesn't want you there? I thought you two were getting along fine."

Nevada could feel a deep blush warming her face. "We were. But things have changed."

Victoria propped her elbows on the desk and studied Nevada with deep concern.

"Really? What sort of things? Did Linc get mad about something? Or did you?"

Nevada massaged her aching forehead with shaky fingers. "This is difficult to explain."

"Nevada, I don't have a clue what this is about, but you've been a nurse long enough to know that patients can be difficult. I'm sure Linc's been a bear at times. But if anyone can deal with it, you can."

Nevada let out a long, pent-up breath. "Well, after Jess called and told him about the fire being arson things changed."

"Oh." Victoria leaned wearily back in the leather chair. "That's not surprising. The fire was a very personal thing for him. Those mares are his life and now he learns that someone targeted them and him. I'm sure the news cut his legs out from under him."

Closing her eyes, Nevada said in a low, strained voice, "Yes. He was upset. He came to my bedroom to tell me about it. And—"

She paused not knowing how to go on,

then she opened her eyes to see Victoria smiling at her.

"And he kissed you," she said happily.

Groaning now, Nevada shook her head. "Oh Victoria, I wish it had only been a kiss. We—we made love. And now things are just terrible between us. It couldn't be more awful. That's why I'm here—to tell you that I can't stay with Linc any longer. It's just too painful. He doesn't want me there."

Without uttering a word, Victoria rose from the chair and came around the desk to put a comforting arm around Nevada's shoulder.

"Oh honey, no wonder you look so miserable. You must be broken-hearted."

Nevada's eyes grew watery as she looked up at Victoria's concerned face. "I never knew anything could hurt this bad, Victoria. I've fallen in love with Linc. But he doesn't want any sort of relationship with me."

Patting her shoulder, Victoria said, "I'm not surprised. Linc has always wanted to be on his own. But I am very disappointed.

You're exactly what he needs in his life. Did he say why he didn't want things to develop between you?"

Wiping her eyes with the back of her hand, Nevada told her, "To put it simply, he doesn't want to go through what his parents went through. Apparently they had a shaky marriage."

"Well, from what Mother told me, Randolf was very possessive and Darla wanted her space. Then there were rumors that Randolf played around and that must have eaten away at her heart."

Nevada's eyes widened at this bit of information. "Does Linc know that?"

Victoria shook her head. "I don't think so. He adored his father. Mother only told me this in total secrecy. And that was long after Randolf had died and Darla had left." Her expression turned earnest. "You won't tell him this, will you, Nevada? I mean, maybe some people would think he ought know the truth of things. But that was so long ago and his mother deserted him. Why pile more heartache on top of that?"

Nevada could see the other woman's reasoning. Yet the idea that Linc didn't know the true facts about his parents' relationship made her chances to have a future with the man practically nil. He was always going to have bitter memories of his mother unless the woman reappeared and explained herself.

"No. I won't tell him. In fact, I won't be telling him anything, except good-bye," she said.

"Oh Nevada," Victoria wailed. "Can't you go back and try to mend fences? At least for another week. By then he ought to be getting his bandages off completely and he'll be able to take care of himself. Right now he needs you."

"Hah!" Nevada said bitterly. "The man doesn't need anyone. Especially me."

"You know that isn't true. He desperately needs your love. He just doesn't know it yet."

Feeling cornered and confused, Nevada jumped to her feet. "I'm going back to the ranch, loading my bags in the car and leaving. You can't change my mind about this, Victoria. I feel badly that I can't finish my end of the bargain. But under circumstances like this I'd hoped you would understand."

Victoria rolled her eyes toward the ceiling. "Oh Nevada, of course I understand. I just wish things could be different. All the way around."

Nevada leaned forward and placed a grateful kiss on Victoria's cheek. "So do I," she whispered tearfully and then turned and hurried out of the office before Victoria could see her break down in sobs.

She drove slowly back to the ranch in hopes the long drive through the countryside would help her pull herself together before she had to face Linc again.

When she arrived, she was thankful not to see him as she hurried to her room to make sure she had everything packed before she carried her bags out to her car.

She was entering the living room, a bag clutched in both hands when Linc stepped out from the kitchen doorway. The moment he spotted her he froze and even from several feet away she could see his eyes narrow.

"What is this?" he asked.

"I think you can figure it out," she said dully. "Your nurse is leaving. You can tear off your bandages—do whatever—I just won't be around to see it."

He crossed the room to where she stood and stared down at her. "What are you doing? You've been here a little more than a week and you're already sick of it?"

His questions caused her to wince. "Don't lay all of that on me, Linc. You know why I'm leaving. And don't act so offended. This is what you want. With me gone, you can breathe a sigh of relief. You won't be tempted to crawl back in bed with me."

His nostrils flared as his gaze searched her face. "Maybe it is for the best," he said flatly. "We sure as hell don't need to keep going on like this."

"I agree," she told him, then with her heart aching, she put on the best professional face she could summon. "Good-bye, Linc. I wish you good luck with your hands and your horses. And I hope whoever tried to hurt you will be caught and punished quickly."

No one could ever hurt him as much as she was doing at this moment, Linc thought. But he understood that her leaving was the best thing, the right thing to do for both of them. He wasn't husband material and Nevada was a woman who deserved a real family. Not a sexual liaison now and then.

Feeling like a wooden statue, he reached out to take her arms. "I'm sorry about this, Nevada. I never set out to hurt you. I hope you'll find another man—someone you can really love."

She pulled away from him. "Really? You like the idea of another man making love to me the way you made love to me?"

Her questions left him sick inside and for a moment he wanted nothing more than to jerk her into his arms and brand her lips with his. But he couldn't touch her in that way now. If he did, the two of them would only wind up in bed again and if that were to happen he would totally and truly be a lost man.

"Good-bye, Nevada," he said thickly, then turned and walked away before the pain in his heart begged her to stay.

A LITTLE MORE than a week later, Nevada was in the tiny room where all the medicine for the clinic was stored. She was searching through a small refrigerator for a certain antibiotic and not having any luck when Victoria entered the room.

"I'm sorry, Victoria. It's not here. I thought we'd ordered it about a month ago. I'll have Joyce look up all the order sheets. Is there a close substitute we can give the patient?"

"Yes." The doctor reached around Nevada's shoulder and picked up a bottle from the refrigerator shelf. "Give him ten cc's of this and make sure you note it on his chart. I'm going to examining room two and see what I can do for Mrs. Parkins."

"She said she vomited for two hours this morning," Nevada said. "What do you think is wrong with her?"

"Betcha ten dollars she's pregnant," Victoria said with a wink. "And I'd win. I've already read the pregnancy test."

Nevada stared at her in surprise. "Mrs. Parkins! She's forty-two years old!"

Victoria threw a hand over her mouth to stifle a laugh. "Nevada! You're a good nurse. You know that any woman whose equipment is in working order is capable of becoming pregnant, no matter what her age."

"Dear God, she's going to be shocked," Nevada muttered.

"Probably. But she'll be happy even more," Victoria said with a smile. "And speaking of happy, how long is it going to be before I see a smile on your face again? You've been going around here looking like you gave yourself a birthday party and nobody came."

Nevada cast her a wry look. "I'm trying, Victoria. I've been telling myself that Linc

Ketchum isn't worth this misery I'm going through. But my heart just doesn't seem to be hearing my words of wisdom."

Victoria sighed with regret. "I know, honey. Before Jess and I got things ironed out, I wasn't fit to be around."

"Yes, but Jess loved you. And both of you did iron out your differences. There's no hope of that with me and Linc."

"I wouldn't say that, Nevada. Not yet. Ross says Linc hasn't been acting like himself at all. That can only mean that he's fretting over you," Victoria reasoned.

While shoving a needle into the bottle of antibiotic Nevada did her best to ignore Victoria's suggestion. There wasn't any point in giving herself any false hope.

"Victoria, do you think if Linc's mother could be found, he might want to see her?"

"I don't know. I've never thought about it too much. She's been gone for so long— since we were all teenagers. And Linc never mentions her at all."

"Because it hurts him too much," Nevada replied. "And frankly, I don't think he's ever going to be able to love any woman until he resolves this idea that she deserted him because she didn't want him."

Frowning thoughtfully, Victoria said, "You could be right."

"I've been thinking, Victoria. And I've been rolling around the idea of trying to find her. What do you think?"

"I wouldn't know where you might start to track her down. I'll ask Ross and Seth if they have any idea." She shoved the cuff of her white lab coat back to glance at her watch. "Right now I've got to get back to work. Mrs. Parkins has been waiting nearly fifteen minutes!"

THAT EVENING AFTER Nevada got off work, she decided to drive by Neil Rankin's law office. She half expected to find the little log building already closed up for the day, but she found the door still open and Connie still sitting at her desk.

The large Hispanic woman with graying black hair smiled broadly at Nevada.

"Well, hello nurse Goodbody," she teased. "What are you up to today?"

"Hi Connie. I need to speak with Neil, if he has a minute to spare," she told the woman.

Connie waved her hand toward the closed door behind her. "Go on in," she told Nevada. "He saw his last client about an hour ago. I think he's just finishing up some paper work before we close up."

"Thanks." Nevada went to the door and rapped on it lightly with her knuckles.

"Come in. I'm fully clothed," Neil called out.

Smiling, Nevada stepped into the lawyer's office. The man was sitting behind a wide oak desk with papers scattered out before him. Wire-rimmed glasses were perched on the end of his nose and his blond hair was rumpled across his forehead. He looked as tired as she felt.

"Hello, Neil. Am I interrupting something important?"

At the sound of her voice, he glanced

up. "Nevada!" he exclaimed. "What a great way to end the day!"

Smiling, she waited for him to skirt the desk and walk over to her. As he reached for both her hands, she understood why people came to him whenever they needed help. He was the sort of man who made you feel comfortable and hopeful.

"What a flatterer you are, Neil Rankin. I'm sure you hand a line to every woman who walks through your door."

He chuckled as he took her by the elbow and led her over to one of two armchairs positioned in front of his desk. "Not *every* woman. At least, only the ones who look like you."

Nevada settled herself in the armchair as Neil walked around the desk and took his own seat.

"So I'm hoping you dropped by to say hello to a friend. I'd hate to think you need legal advice."

Nevada shook her head. "Not legal advice. But I do need help. And I didn't know anyone else to turn to."

He studied her with interest. "Well, I'm glad you have that much confidence in me. I don't know if it's really warranted, but shoot your problem at me anyway and I'll try."

Scooting to the edge of the chair she leaned toward his desk. "I want you to help me find someone. A person who used to live here. On the T Bar K, actually."

Instantly, Neil's brows lifted with curiosity. "On the ranch? But surely Victoria could help you with that problem."

"No. She doesn't have a clue about this woman. She's going to talk to her brothers, but I seriously doubt that they know any more than she does."

Neil reached for a pen and scooted a yellow legal pad to the center of his desk. "Does this woman have a name?"

"Darla Ketchum. Darla Ketchum Carlton to be exact."

Neil reared back in his chair. "That's Linc's mother!"

Nevada's head bobbed up and down. "Yes. I want to find her—for him."

A low whistle passed the lawyer's lips. "Boy, maybe you need to think this over, Nevada. Darla Ketchum is a touchy subject. Especially where Linc is concerned."

Nevada grimaced. "You don't have to tell me that. We—uh—we already had a discussion about her and the reasons why she left the ranch."

Neil shrugged. "Well, from what I understand the woman remarried shortly after Randolf died."

"Do you know who the man she married was? Did he live here?"

Neil rubbed his chin thoughtfully. "If I recall right, he wasn't from around here. Because I remember Ross saying something about the man coming up from Texas in a big black limousine. He was just so relieved that Linc wasn't in that car when it left the ranch." He cast her a wry smile. "Funny how those sorts of things stick with kids. And that's what we were at the time, just kids. I might have been sixteen or seventeen and Linc a fraction younger."

How tragic, Nevada thought, for Linc

to lose his father and his mother within a short period of time and the loss had occurred when he'd been at such a young, impressionable age. No wonder loneliness had shaped and molded his life.

"Such a long time ago," Nevada said wistfully. "I wonder why he has never been able to ever let go."

"Of his mother's leaving?" Neil asked.

Nevada nodded. "He believes she deliberately deserted him. That she quit communicating with him just to spite him for not leaving the ranch with her."

"Hmm. That's some heavy stuff there, Nevada. I'm not sure we should even try to intervene."

Nevada scooted to the very edge of her seat as her eyes pleaded with the lawyer. "That's the whole problem. No one has been brave enough to confront Linc about this problem. They've allowed him to bottle it all up and try to sweep the whole incident under the rug. The man lost his father and then his mother vanished from his life. Don't you think he deserves to know the truth of the matter? Don't you think it would help him come to terms with issues that he refuses to face?"

Neil held his palms up. "Look, Nevada, I totally agree with you. But I'd like to know why you've taken on this task. I wasn't aware that you were that closely acquainted with Linc."

Nevada's gaze dropped to her folded hands. "I wasn't acquainted with him until I became his nurse. I guess you weren't aware that I went out to the ranch to care for him after he was released from the hospital."

"I'd heard he was home and doing well. I'd been meaning to drive out for a little visit, but I've been tied up with all sorts of clients. And I had to be out of town all of last week." With a thoughtful look at her, he tapped his pen against the legal pad. "What happened with you and Linc? You got close and he started running backwards?"

Relieved that he understood without her

having to explain any embarrassing details, she nodded. "That's it, exactly."

"You must care for him a lot to go to this much trouble to find his mother."

"Very much."

Neil leaned forward and gave her an encouraging smile. "Well, give me what information you have and I'll see what I can do. I'm not a detective, Nevada. So don't expect miracles. But I do have a few friends around the country who work on missing-persons cases."

"I'll be grateful for any sort of help," Nevada told him. "But maybe I should ask how much this sort of thing will cost me. I do have some savings put away. If that's not enough I could take out a loan—"

He lifted a hand to halt her words. "Nevada, that's the last thing you need to be worried about. I don't intend to charge you anything. And as for my contacts, they all enjoy a challenge."

Nevada grimaced. "Yes, but I'm sure they like money, too. They can't make a living giving away their services."

"Believe me, honey, none of them are hurting. They have plenty of rich clients to keep them afloat. You know the sort— spoiled kids who run away from home have to be found."

She breathed a sigh of relief. "All right, if you say so. I won't worry about the money part."

Tossing down his pen, Neil smiled at her with disbelief. "You know, sometimes you women amaze me. I don't understand why you're willing to do so much for us nasty men."

"I care about Linc," she reasoned.

His expression turned to one of wry appreciation. "Yeah. So much so that you're willing to lose all your savings and go in debt for the man."

She drew in a deep breath and blew it out. "I happen to think he's worth it."

Neil chuckled. "You know what, I happen to think he's worth it, too."

Chapter Thirteen

Almost two weeks later, as midnight approached, Miss Lori went into labor. For several nights running Linc had been sitting up with the mare to give Skinny a rest. But tonight Skinny had refused to go to bed. The old wrangler had predicted the full moon would start the mare's birthing engine, and he'd been right.

Easing out of the chair he'd propped against the wall, Linc went over to where Skinny was half sitting, half lying in a bed of straw. He gently shook the old man's shoulder.

"Skinny, wake up. Miss Lori has started."

For a moment the old man looked around in a dazed stupor until he spotted the mare wringing her tail and bending her nose around to her side.

"Hot damn! Has she laid down yet?"

"Once. Then she bounced back up."

Bones creaked and popped as the old man rose to his feet and rubbed his hands together with excited glee. "It won't be long now! Bet it's going to be a black filly with a star on her forehead."

Linc smiled wryly at the old wrangler. "That's a big stretch. Miss Lori is black with a star on her forehead."

Chuckling, Skinny hopped along on his one good knee until he reached the mare's side. Linc watched as his old friend carefully rubbed his hand over the mare's belly and flank. The man never wanted to miss any of the foals being born. It was a very special time for him, just as it always was for Linc.

A LITTLE MORE than an hour later, the foal was born and as Skinny had predicted it was a black filly with a star on its face. The birth had gone smoothly and the two men had had little more to do than to stand back and watch the miracle in process.

In a matter of minutes after the birth, the mare was on her feet cleaning the little filly of lingering afterbirth. An hour later, the baby was standing up on her long legs, nudging her mother's flank in search of sweet, nourishing milk.

Skinny cackled with pleasure and slapped Linc on the shoulder. "She's a beauty, Linc. You got a good one on her feet."

"It wasn't just me that got her here, Skinny. You and all the other guys are the reason we have one of the best remudas in six states." He patted Skinny's arm. "Now what do you say me and you go have a cup of coffee?"

The two men slipped into the back of the bunkhouse where the kitchen was located. Linc boiled coffee on the stove and the two men sat at the long table and carefully sipped the steaming brew.

Skinny rattled on about the new filly until he realized that Linc wasn't saying much about anything. The old wrangler set his cup on the wooden table and studied Linc with his faded blue eyes.

"What's the matter with you, boy? Hell, it's been nearly twelve months since we bred Miss Lori. And all that time you've been watching her like a proud papa. I figured you'd be dancing a jig right about now."

Linc rolled his eyes. "Skinny, when have you ever seen me dance? Never. And there isn't anything wrong with me. I'm happy. The filly is great. She's going to be beautiful and smart and tough. What more do you want me to say?"

Skinny shook his head and mumbled into his cup.

"What was that?" Linc asked.

Lifting his head, Skinny scowled at him. "Nothin'. I just thought—well, I thought now that you've got to come back to work, that things would be different. Like they used to be. I've known you since you were a little tot in diapers. But you aren't that same boy."

Sighing with frustration, Linc left his

seat and went over to the cabinets. As he searched around for some leftovers to snack on, he said, "Damn it, Skinny, it wasn't too long ago that these hands of mine were fried. And I was lucky that I hadn't been killed. That does something to a man."

"And whose fault was that?" Skinny shot back at him. "Nobody told you to be a hero and rescue all those mares. The boys in the bunkhouse were coming to help you. If you'd only waited—"

"None of the mares would still be alive," Linc finished sharply. "And the bastard who set the fire is still out there, getting away with near murder. But you expect me to be myself?"

He found half of an apple pie in the refrigerator, whacked out a piece and carried it in his hand over to the table. While he ate, Skinny folded his arms across his chest and looked disgusted.

"If I was you, I don't think I'd be tryin' to blame my behavior on nearly bein' burned to death. Yeah, the thought of that is enough to curl a man's toes, but that ain't your real problem and we both know it."

The pie in Linc's hand stopped midway to his mouth. "What the hell are you talking about now, Skinny? And since when did you become such a psychologist?"

Skinny pushed back his brown felt hat and scrunched up his wrinkled face. "I don't know what that fancy word is and I don't care to know. But a one-eyed man could see you're missin' that pretty little nurse something awful."

Linc started to yell at the old man that he was going senile, but instead, he crammed the remainder of the pie in his mouth and tried to ignore him.

It didn't work. Skinny started again. "She was a nice girl, Linc. Too nice for the likes of you, I guess."

"That's right," Linc said curtly. "She went on to greener pastures."

"Well, I can't blame her. You didn't have much to offer her. Look at yourself. What are you anyway, forty years old now? With her being so young and fresh, she probably thought you were just a few years away from the nursing home."

"I'm thirty-eight, Skinny. And I'm hardly over the hill."

"Well, not like me. Course not. But a young woman like her wants kids of her own. Can't get 'em with a man that goes to sleep every night in a rocking chair."

Linc didn't want to think about Nevada having children or having sex or even touching a man. He didn't want to think of Nevada at all. But for the past two weeks since she'd left, he had not been able to focus his attention on anything. She was always there in his mind, consuming every part of it until he thought he was going crazy.

"All right, old man. I've heard enough of this. You can sit here and keep yapping if you want to. I'm going to bed."

As Linc started to rise from the table, Skinny said, "Where you going to sleep tonight? Going back up to your folks' old house?"

"What if I am?" Linc asked curtly.

"How come?" Skinny asked in a goading voice. "Think that little nurse is going to come back and make you feel better?"

Gritting his teeth, Linc rinsed his cup out and turned it upside down in the sink.

"No. And I don't want her to!"

"You're a damn liar, Linc Ketchum."

No one had ever dared to call him such a thing and it shocked him that Skinny, his best buddy, and a man who had been like an uncle to him all of his life could insult him like this.

Turning slowly away from the sink, Linc walked back over to where Skinny sat with his hat pushed back on his forehead and his chin thrust stubbornly forward.

"Look, Skinny, it's like you said. I don't have anything to offer the woman. And once she found that out—well, I'd be just like my father. Miserable."

Skinny blinked, then swallowed down the last of his coffee. "No, ain't no way you could be like Randolf. You just ain't made that way."

Funny that Skinny should say such a

thing, Linc thought. Everyone had always told him he had mannerisms and a personality just like his father's. "What's that supposed to mean? I can't read your mind."

Skinny wiped a hand across his mouth as though he wished he'd done a bit more thinking before he'd spoken. "Well, it just means that he was different than you. That's all. And it was your mother that carried the misery around. Not your father."

Frowning, Linc sat back down at the table and looked at Skinny. "Don't you think I know that? She was yelling to Dad every day about this dusty, isolated ranch. She wanted away from here and she made him miserable because he wouldn't take her."

Skinny made a tsking noise with his tongue. "Guess I shouldn't have said anything, boy. But seems like you're all messed up about things. And I don't want to see you lose that pretty little nurse. She looked at you like a woman who'd love you 'til the day she died. A man can't find that every day."

Linc didn't have to hear that from Skinny to know it was the truth. He'd been around women all his adult life. He'd shared their company and their beds. But not one of them had touched him the way Nevada had touched him. She'd gilded his heart with sweet honey, she'd lifted away the heavy loneliness inside him and made him wish for little ones sitting around the breakfast table, riding his shoulders and calling him Daddy. Made him dream of nights with Nevada in his arms, making love to him until the end of their days.

"You're right, Skinny," he said finally. "Nevada is one of a kind. But I can't ask her to live here on the ranch with me. She would eventually get sick of the dust, the isolation, the long hours I'd have to give to the horses and not her. She'd want to leave just like my mother and then where would I be?"

"Look, boy, if you think—" He stopped, lifted his hat and scratched the top of his head. "Darla didn't want to leave the ranch because of those things. Oh, she said them enough to your father, I'm sure. But Randolf knew the real reason and he didn't care. As long as he got what he wanted that's all that mattered to him. I guess in that way he was just like Tucker."

Linc was taken completely aback and he stared at Skinny as though the old man had just suffered a stroke. "What's the matter with you, Skinny? Everyone you ask would tell you that Randolf was not like Tucker. Tucker was a tough, indifferent man. Especially to his wife. He was a philanderer, a womanizer and he liked his Kentucky bourbon. Dad was not like that."

"He wasn't? Or was he just careful enough to keep it all hid? He was just as much a Ketchum as Tucker ever was. They were brothers and they shared the same hot blood. Randolf was more easygoing than Tucker. That much is true. But other than that they were two peas in a pod. If your Daddy hadn't gotten sick with his heart you would have seen for yourself. Before that, you were too young to know what was really going on with your folks."

Stricken by this revelation, Linc reached over and snatched a hold on Skinny's sleeve. "Are you telling me the truth?"

"I've never lied to you before," Skinny said flatly. "Ain't about to start now."

Linc felt sick as all the air drained out of his lungs. "Then why didn't you tell me this before?"

Skinny shook his head. "Wasn't any need to. You always thought highly of your daddy and I didn't want to make you think any less."

"Yes, but you let me go on thinking that my mother—that all their troubles were her fault!"

"Linc, I ain't never been married. But I had a woman once and lost her in an accident. I'm old and maybe you think I don't know about love or any of that stuff. But I do. And I can tell you that there's always two sides to everything."

Linc rose from the table and wiped a weary hand across his face. "She wanted me to go with her. After Dad died, she wanted me to start a new life with her. I didn't want to go. I thought she was de-manding. I thought she'd made Dad so miserable it had ruined his heart. But I didn't go. I hurt her for sure. And now—" He shook his head and started to-ward the door. "I don't want to talk about this anymore, Skinny," he said hoarsely. "I'm going back to the barn."

HOURS LATER, LINC was in the foaling pen, lying on a mound of straw as he watched the new filly toddle after her mother. The baby's black hair was dry now and her legs were straighter. Her little black mane stuck straight up like a punk rocker's hair and each time she walked near Linc she gave him a sassy shake of her head.

If he hadn't felt so rotten, he would have laughed at the filly's antics. But tonight he felt as if his heart had dropped to the bot-tom of a rocky canyon. He'd thought all along that getting back to work and being able to use his hands would make him a happy man. But it hadn't turned out that way. The job he'd always loved wasn't giving him the same joy he'd felt before the fire and he had to admit to himself, if not to Skinny, that Nevada was the reason.

He would never have believed that he could miss anyone so much. But after she'd packed up and left, the house had felt like a tomb. Only he hadn't been dead; he'd only felt dead.

Long after she was gone, the sound of her laugh and her sweet voice calling to him had seemed to ricochet off the walls. After the second night, he'd packed up his things and returned to the bunkhouse. At least there Cook had been able to give him a helping hand whenever he needed something. And the conversation of the ranch hands made him feel less lonely.

But nothing felt the same as it had before Nevada came into his life. And now he had to deal with the notion that all the arguments he'd given her for staying apart had been wrong. He'd been wrong. All these years and all the bitterness he'd felt for his mother had painted his image of her as very dark. And he'd transferred that darkness over to Nevada, simply because he'd been afraid of being hurt.

Oh God, how wrong he'd been.

"Linc? You awake?"

At the sound of Skinny's low voice, Linc lifted his head to see the man entering the horse stall. A pen light illuminated his path as he approached the pile of straw where Linc was trying to rest.

"What the hell are you doing out here, Skinny? It's three o'clock in the morning! You should be in bed."

Skinny finally reached Linc's side. There he squatted on his boot heels and dangled his hands between his knees. "I went to bed," he said. "But I couldn't sleep. I felt too ashamed of myself. I—"

"Skinny," Linc interrupted, only to have the old man barge in.

"No, Linc. Let me say my piece. I'm sorry about all that I said back there in the bunkhouse. I shouldn't have. I should have kept my mouth shut. You are just like a son to me. The son I always wanted. I just want you to be happy. And I thought—well—I thought you loved that little gal and that you just needed a nudge her way. I didn't mean to spill all that about your folks."

Pushing himself to a sitting position, Linc reached over and gripped Skinny's forearm. "Don't apologize, Skinny. You did the right thing and I thank you for it. Really thank you for it."

"You mean that?" Skinny asked, his voice full of worried doubt.

Linc chuckled as his heart came to a certain and sudden decision. "You're a bold old codger, you know it? One of these days I'm going to have to name my first son after you. And I don't intend to call him Skinny. So you might as well get ready to cough up your real name and let everybody finally know what it is."

Skinny cackled and patted Linc on the shoulder. "Don't worry, boy. When the time comes, I'll let you know."

THE NEXT MORNING Nevada had just gotten out of the shower when the telephone rang and she moaned with loud frustration. She only had twenty minutes to get her hair dried, her makeup and clothes on and drive to work. She didn't have time for small talk.

Wrapping a towel around her wet hair, she snatched up the receiver. "Hello," she said in a breathless rush.

"Nevada, it's Neil here. Do you have a minute? I wanted to catch you before you left for work."

Nevada's heart began to hammer with anticipation. Two weeks had passed since she'd gone to Neil's office and asked the lawyer for help in finding Darla Ketchum. Since then she hadn't heard any news about the search.

"You've found Linc's mother?" she asked quickly.

"No. Not yet. But we have made a little progress. We found out that her husband is dead and has been for many years. We thought we might be able to locate some of his relatives, but so far we haven't been able to. And as for Darla's relatives, she must have been a black sheep of the family or something. She doesn't appear to be related to anyone that we can find in San Antonio."

Nevada felt deflated, but she told herself that things like this sometimes took months or years. She couldn't expect instant results. And even if Neil managed to find Darla this very day, she didn't know if it would help matters with Linc. She could only hope.

So far, Nevada hadn't heard a word from him. And that really hadn't surprised her. But she'd been hoping and praying he would have a change of heart and realize the two of them were meant to be together.

"Well, at least that's a start," she conceded. "I've been talking to Victoria and Marina and from what they say no one in the family has heard from her. Not since Linc had his last contact with her and that was years ago, shortly after she left the ranch."

Neil said, "Don't worry, Nevada. We'll pick up a trace somewhere, somehow. In the meantime, have you talked with Linc?"

Tears suddenly blurred her eyes and she hated herself for being so emotional and weak. But any thought of Linc crushed her with sadness. "No. As far as I know he hasn't made any effort to contact me." She sighed. "I suppose most people would tell me I'm crazy and that I should give up and forget about the man. But I can't, Neil. Does that make any sense to you?"

"Honey, from what I can see, love doesn't ever make sense. And it's pretty damn hard to find. Hang on 'til you can't hang on any more. That's what I say."

She blinked at the tears spilling over her eyelids. "Thank you, Neil. Let me know if you discover anything at all."

He promised he would, then hung up the phone. Nevada wiped her eyes and hurried to the bathroom to dry her hair.

She'd tossed the towel from her head and was about to push the button on the blow dryer when she heard the doorbell ring.

The interruption put a weary scowl on her face as she hurried to the front door. Not one of her friends ever stopped by at this hour in the morning. The caller had to be the landlord. He'd been promising to get Nevada new carpet for the past year. Maybe he was finally going to come through, she thought skeptically.

"All right. Just a moment," she called through the door as another ring sounded.

Knowing that the glass storm door was safely latched behind the main wooden door, she didn't take the time to peek out the peephole at the caller. Instead, she swung the panel of wood to one side and then stared with an open mouth.

"Linc!" she finally gasped.

In all of her imaginings, she'd never expected him to show up at her apartment like this with his hat in his hands and a humble look on his face. The sight was enough to make her hands fumble helplessly with the latch on the storm door before she finally managed to open it.

"Hello, Nevada. May I come in?"

Her throat was suddenly so thick she could hardly speak. Sweet, deep emotions began to fill her heart and spill over into the rest of her body like the waterfall where they'd hidden from the storm.

"Of course, Linc."

She pushed the door wider and he stepped past her and into the small apartment.

Nervously, Nevada turned to face him. "I—you'll have to excuse me," she said as she touched a hand to her wet, tangled hair. "I just got out of the shower and I'm still a mess."

He stepped toward her and she noticed his hands wrapped tightly around the brown felt hat. They were free of bandages now and thick scars from the fire were quite evident. Even so, his hands were a beautiful sight to Nevada.

"You look great," he said quietly. "Really great."

Her gaze settled on his rugged face. "So do you," she murmured,

In a nervous gesture, his fingers began to smooth around the brim of his hat. "Uh—I guess you're getting ready to go to work. I wasn't thinking, I'm interrupting."

Nevada's heart suddenly felt so full of anticipation she thought it was going to burst. "Victoria will understand. That's the good thing about having a boss like her."

"She's a pretty good cousin, too," Linc said fondly.

Nevada nodded and then she couldn't stand it any longer. She closed the last few steps between them. "Linc, what are you doing here?"

A groan sounded in his throat as he reached up and raked one hand through his dark hair. "I don't know how to start, or what to say to you. I feel like a damn idiot and I'm sure I look even worse."

"You look tired," she said honestly.

"I've been up all night. Miss Lori finally had her baby last night. A little black filly with a white star."

Nevada had to smile. "That's good. Congratulations."

His expression remained sober. "Miss Lori isn't why I didn't get any sleep though. I haven't been able to sleep much at all since you left," he admitted. "I—"

"Linc," she interrupted, only to have him toss his hat aside and reach for her shoulders.

"Just wait, Nevada. Wait and hear me out. I know you probably want to curse me up one side and down the other. I wouldn't blame you if you hated my guts now. But I'm hoping against hope that you're a forgiving woman."

Hope surged in her heart and that organ began to beat as though it had wings and was soaring higher and higher.

"Why?" she asked simply.

His features twisted with regret. "Because I've been wrong. And stupid. And a few other things that I don't care to repeat."

She looked at him with helpless confusion. "I don't understand, Linc. You said we couldn't be together. You said—"

"I said too many damn things that didn't do anything but hurt both of us," he admitted.

Tentatively, her hands lifted and framed his dear face. "What exactly are you trying to say to me, Linc? I don't understand this change."

With a muffled sound, he tugged her into his arms and buried his face in her damp hair. "I'm trying to say I love you, Nevada."

She shook her head in dazed wonder. "But you were so against that."

"I've learned a lot these past two weeks, Nevada. One is that you can't dictate what your heart feels. It has a mind of its own. I loved you in spite of myself. Living without you has been horrible. And I've come to see that I do want all the things that other men have. A wife and kids, a family that loves me. I was always so afraid of that idea. Afraid that it would turn out like my parents' marriage and then I would be hurt even worse than I was by them. But I've come to realize that I have to move past all that now. I'm different from my dad and you're not Darla. I think we can be happy. What do you think?"

He pulled back his head to look at her and tears of pure joy slipped down Nevada's cheeks as she gazed upon the love in his eyes.

"I *know* we'll be happy, Linc. We both understand how important family is, how necessary it is for children to have two parents who truly love each other. That's why we'll try even harder to do things right."

His eyes glazed over as his arms tightened around her and his head bent down to hers. "Something tells me we won't have to try too hard," he whispered. "I think loving each other is going to come natural."

Nevada couldn't have agreed more and she raised on tiptoe to meet the sweet promise of his kiss. And for long moments their lips searched, their hands clung with need.

Linc was the one who finally lifted his head and presented her with a dazzling smile that took Nevada's breath away. "Go dry your hair and get dressed. We have things to do today. Do you think Victoria will give you the day off?"

"I don't know," she said with a happy laugh. "If my usual replacement will come in, then she will."

"I'll call her right now," Linc said as his gaze darted around the room in search of a phone. "You go get ready. We've got a date with the county clerk to get our marriage license."

He pushed her out of his embrace and turned her toward the door leading out of the small living area, but she quickly whirled back to him.

"Marriage license! Linc! You can't be in that big a hurry. I want us to be married in church with all the beautiful trimmings! You will give me that much, won't you?" she pleaded.

His expression softened and for the first time in his life he knew what it was like to spoil and love and protect a woman. His woman.

"Of course I will, honey. I want us to have a nice wedding, too. Just so you don't make me wait too long. We can still get the license today. It'll keep."

She started to stand on her tiptoes to kiss him again. But at that moment another thought struck her and she looked at him worriedly.

"Linc, uh—maybe before we make any plans I need to confess something to you."

Amusement crinkled his green eyes. "What is it? That you have a passion for stabbing people with needles? I already knew that," he teased.

"No, Linc. I'm serious. I've done something that you should know about." She paused long enough to draw in a bracing breath. "It's about your mother."

A frown puckered his brows and Nevada could only wonder if she'd ruined everything.

"My mother? I don't understand."

"After I left the ranch I was pretty upset. I decided there wouldn't be much chance for us unless something changed your mind. I was hoping to find your mother so that the two of you might work out your differences. I asked Neil Rankin to help me search for her." She reached for his hand and pressed it lovingly between hers. "No matter what you think, Linc, I can't believe that she simply turned her back on you."

He didn't say anything, and Nevada's heart sank as he lowered his head and shook it back and forth.

"Are you angry with me?" she asked after several minutes passed.

Lifting his head, he looked at her with moist eyes. "I'm not angry, darling. I'm floored that you would go to such lengths for me. And I don't think I deserve a woman like you. But I'm going to try like hell to be deserving. Just give me a chance."

She let out a relieved breath. "I was afraid. You've been so bitter about her. And—"

Linc lifted a forefinger to her lips. "There's something I need to tell you, honey. I had an enlightening conversation with Skinny. And it seems that things were not what I thought they were between my parents. Apparently my father wasn't faithful and my mother was very unhappy about it. That's why she wanted to leave the ranch. She wanted the two of us to start over somewhere else." His mouth twisted with regret. "I guess my dad couldn't give up his vices."

"And your mother loved him too much to leave," she added. "Oh, Linc, I'm so sorry. But maybe now if we can find her things could be different for the two of you."

He smiled gently down at her. "My hands are still scarred, but not my heart, my darling. If we're able to track down Mom's whereabouts, I'll be glad. But right now I've found the woman I'm going to love for the rest of my life."

Her eyes were bright with happy tears as she lifted his hand to her lips. "Can we live in your parents' house, Linc? And turn it into a real home?"

"It's waiting for us and all the children we're going to have. And maybe someday, if we do find Mom, we'll be able to present her with grandchildren."

Suddenly, dressing and work and marriage license were put on the back burner as Linc's hands pushed the blue terry robe Nevada was wearing down off her naked body.

"Oh—by the way," he murmured against the curve of her shoulder. "I think I'd better warn you that I've promised Skinny to name our first boy after him."

She giggled. "Skinny?"

"Yeah. But he'll tell us his real name when the times comes."

And that time would come soon, Nevada thought happily. Very soon.

* * * * *

YES! Please send me the *Cowboy at Heart* collection in Larger Print. This collection begins with 3 FREE books and 2 FREE gifts in the first shipment, and more free gifts will follow! My books will arrive in 8 monthly shipments until I have the entire 51-book *Cowboy at Heart* collection. I will receive 2 or 3 FREE books in each shipment and I will pay just $4.99 U.S./ $5.89 CDN. for each of the other four books in each shipment, plus $2.99 for shipping and handling.* If I decide to keep the entire collection, I'll have paid for only 32 books because 19 books are FREE! I understand that by accepting the 3 free books and gifts places me under no obligation to buy anything. I can always return a shipment and cancel at any time. My free books and gifts are mine to keep no matter what I decide.

256 HCN 0779   456 HCN 0779

Name _____ (PLEASE PRINT)

Address _____ Apt. #

City _____ State/Prov. _____ Zip/Postal Code

Signature (if under 18, a parent or guardian must sign)

Mail to the Harlequin® Reader Service:

IN U.S.A.: P.O. Box 1867, Buffalo, NY 14240-1867
IN CANADA: P.O. Box 609, Fort Erie, Ontario L2A 5X3

* Terms and prices subject to change without notice. Prices do not include applicable taxes. Sales tax applicable in N.Y. Canadian residents will be charged applicable taxes. This offer is limited to one order per household. All orders subject to approval. Credit or debit balances in a customer's account(s) may be offset by any other outstanding balance owed by or to the customer. Please allow 4 to 6 weeks for delivery. Offer available while quantities last. Offer not available to Quebec residents.

Your Privacy—The Harlequin® Reader Service is committed to protecting your privacy. Our Privacy Policy is available online at www.ReaderService.com or upon request from the Harlequin Reader Service.

We make a portion of our mailing list available to reputable third parties that offer products we believe may interest you. If you prefer that we not exchange your name with third parties, or if you wish to clarify or modify your communication preferences, please visit us at www.ReaderService.com/consumerschoice or write to us at Harlequin Reader Service Preference Service, P.O. Box 9062, Buffalo, NY 14269. Include your complete name and address.

CAHBPA13

REQUEST YOUR FREE BOOKS!
2 FREE NOVELS PLUS 2 FREE GIFTS!

✦ HARLEQUIN

American ★ Romance®

LOVE, HOME & HAPPINESS

YES! Please send me 2 FREE Harlequin® American Romance® novels and my 2 FREE gifts (gifts are worth about $10). After receiving them, if I don't wish to receive any more books, I can return the shipping statement marked "cancel." If I don't cancel, I will receive 4 brand-new novels every month and be billed just $4.49 per book in the U.S. or $5.24 per book in Canada. That's a savings of at least 14% off the cover price! It's quite a bargain! Shipping and handling is just 50¢ per book in the U.S. and 75¢ per book in Canada.* I understand that accepting the 2 free books and gifts places me under no obligation to buy anything. I can always return a shipment and cancel at any time. Even if I never buy another book, the two free books and gifts are mine to keep forever.

154/354 HDN FV47

Name	(PLEASE PRINT)

Address	Apt. #

City	State/Prov.	Zip/Postal Code

Signature (if under 18, a parent or guardian must sign)

Mail to the Harlequin® Reader Service:
IN U.S.A.: P.O. Box 1867, Buffalo, NY 14240-1867
IN CANADA: P.O. Box 609, Fort Erie, Ontario L2A 5X3

Want to try two free books from another line?
Call 1-800-873-8635 or visit www.ReaderService.com.

* Terms and prices subject to change without notice. Prices do not include applicable taxes. Sales tax applicable in N.Y. Canadian residents will be charged applicable taxes. Offer not valid in Quebec. This offer is limited to one order per household. Not valid for current subscribers to Harlequin American Romance books. All orders subject to credit approval. Credit or debit balances in a customer's account(s) may be offset by any other outstanding balance owed by or to the customer. Please allow 4 to 6 weeks for delivery. Offer available while quantities last.

Your Privacy—The Harlequin® Reader Service is committed to protecting your privacy. Our Privacy Policy is available online at www.ReaderService.com or upon request from the Harlequin Reader Service.

We make a portion of our mailing list available to reputable third parties that offer products we believe may interest you. If you prefer that we not exchange your name with third parties, or if you wish to clarify or modify your communication preferences, please visit us at www.ReaderService.com/consumerschoice or write to us at Harlequin Reader Service Preference Service, P.O. Box 9062, Buffalo, NY 14269. Include your complete name and address.

HARDIR13

REQUEST YOUR FREE BOOKS!
2 FREE NOVELS PLUS 2 FREE GIFTS!

HARLEQUIN®

super romance®

Exciting, emotional, unexpected!

YES! Please send me 2 FREE Harlequin® Superromance® novels and my 2 FREE gifts (gifts are worth about $10). After receiving them, if I don't wish to receive any more books, I can return the shipping statement marked "cancel." If I don't cancel, I will receive 6 brand-new novels every month and be billed just $4.69 per book in the U.S. or $5.24 per book in Canada. That's a savings of at least 15% off the cover price! It's quite a bargain! Shipping and handling is just 50¢ per book in the U.S. and 75¢ per book in Canada.* I understand that accepting the 2 free books and gifts places me under no obligation to buy anything. I can always return a shipment and cancel at any time. Even if I never buy another book, the two free books and gifts are mine to keep forever.

135/336 HDN FV5K

Name	(PLEASE PRINT)	

Address		Apt. #

City	State/Prov.	Zip/Postal Code

Signature (if under 18, a parent or guardian must sign)

Mail to the **Harlequin® Reader Service:**
IN U.S.A.: P.O. Box 1867, Buffalo, NY 14240-1867
IN CANADA: P.O. Box 609, Fort Erie, Ontario L2A 5X3

**Are you a current subscriber to Harlequin Superromance books and want to receive the larger-print edition?
Call 1-800-873-8635 or visit www.ReaderService.com.**

* Terms and prices subject to change without notice. Prices do not include applicable taxes. Sales tax applicable in N.Y. Canadian residents will be charged applicable taxes. Offer not valid in Quebec. This offer is limited to one order per household. Not valid for current subscribers to Harlequin Superromance books. All orders subject to credit approval. Credit or debit balances in a customer's account(s) may be offset by any other outstanding balance owed by or to the customer. Please allow 4 to 6 weeks for delivery. Offer available while quantities last.

Your Privacy—The Harlequin® Reader Service is committed to protecting your privacy. Our Privacy Policy is available online at www.ReaderService.com or upon request from the Harlequin Reader Service.

We make a portion of our mailing list available to reputable third parties that offer products we believe may interest you. If you prefer that we not exchange your name with third parties, or if you wish to clarify or modify your communication preferences, please visit us at www.ReaderService.com/consumerchoice or write to us at Harlequin Reader Service Preference Service, P.O. Box 9062, Buffalo, NY 14269. Include your complete name and address.

HSRDIR13

ReaderService.com

Manage your account online!

- Review your order history
- Manage your payments
- Update your address

---

*We've designed
the Harlequin® Reader Service
website just for you.*

Enjoy all the features!

- Reader excerpts from any series
- Respond to mailings and
  special monthly offers
- Discover new series available to you
- Browse the Bonus Bucks catalog
- Share your feedback

Visit us at:
ReaderService.com

RS13